WATERFORD

# FOLK
# TALES

T0353246

# WATERFORD
# FOLK
# TALES

ANNE FARRELL

ILLUSTRATED BY

JASON COOKE

*This book is dedicated to the memory of a beautiful soul and brilliant mind, my lovely daughter-in-law Elaine, wife and soulmate of Brendan and mother to Rory and Eimear*

First published 2013, reprinted 2017

The History Press Ireland
50 City Quay
Dublin 2
Ireland
www.thehistorypress.ie

British Library Cataloguing in Publication Data.
A catalogue record for this book is available from the British Library.

ISBN 978 1 84588 757 5

Typesetting and origination by The History Press

Printed and bound by TJ International Ltd, Padstow, Cornwall

# Contents

# ACKNOWLEDGEMENTS

My grateful thanks to Liam Murphy, master storyteller, for all his help and encouragement; Julian Walton, folklorist; the late Denny Maher; the late Patrick and Eileen Kirwan for keeping tradition alive; Lord Waterford; Breda Mears; Noel McDonagh; Richard Power; Christy Brophy; the late Michael Carberry and the Ballyduff Parish Council; Mary the Memory; Jack Burtchaell; Portlaw Heritage Centre, and to all the other people who gave me their time and kindness.

Thank you – *Diolch yn fawr* – to Myles Pepper, Jane and Gethin Griffiths, for making the Wales/Waterford connection possible.

My thanks also to neighbours Elaine Mullan, Ian McHardy and Hazel Farrell who kept me on track.

Finally thanks to my family and particularly my lovely husband Brendan, who has been patience itself since the start of this project.

# INTRODUCTION

I was born into a family who always told stories, so I had no choice but to be aware of that other life which dances just out of sight.

Storytelling is a delight to the soul for it shifts and changes like the wind and what you started out to tell, more often than not, will end up being a different story altogether.

Sometimes when you sit in front of an audience the stories you planned to tell do not seem right. I never know until I get there what to tell. It is something subtle in the relationship between audience and storyteller. I have always been lucky in my choices when I trusted my instinct. Many times people have come and thanked me because they believed that the story was not only for them but about them. Life is wonderful.

When you think you know a lot about storytelling, you can be brought back to earth with a bump. Many years ago I did storytelling tours in Wales with Liam Murphy and we visited a Community Care Home in St David's regularly. When we returned one time, after a year away, a young man called Christian asked if he could tell his story, as he had been practising for the whole year. We gladly moved over and he sat between us. His telling of his own story, from the first time he came to the home up until the day we came telling stories, nearly broke our hearts. A speech impediment hampered him but he wanted to let us know that we had changed his life. Everyone cried and rejoiced at the same time. A whole year spent practising one story totally amazed us.

Everyone has a story, if you only take time to listen.

One of the most startling things I discovered when I began writing this book was that local stories are bred into the bones of us. There is no 'source', as demanded by academia; we have just known them since we were children at our parents' knees.

The stories in this collection are about many different areas in Co. Waterford and it has been a joy to chase them up. Some are tales I regularly tell and have a fondness for. *An Bídeach* and *Slabhra na Fírinne* – The Chain of Truth are favourites in the country areas while in the city people like Aoife and Strongbow, Crotty the Highwayman, The Tunnel beneath the Suir and The Republican Pig. It is all a matter of what you can get your imagination working on and local knowledge is a great spur.

I always ask for guidance before telling a story and firmly believe that I have a host of helpers nudging the right story to the forefront of my mind. Amergin, mentioned in The Three Sisters, was a druid and bard and is always on the edge of my thinking. What a book he could have written.

Storytelling is different from reading or writing a story, and I have told these stories in the manner of 'telling'. I hope it does not mar your enjoyment. Put your own *blás* on them and swing them this way and that in your mind. Let the voices you hear be of your own creation.

## One

# AOIFE AND STRONGBOW

*This story began in another county but has always had a place in the hearts of the people of Waterford. That it is based in historical, traceable fact makes it all the more real and special. The River Suir, which Aoife saw when she came here, still flows by the city quays. Standing on the end of the quay, near the Tower Hotel, is Reginald's Tower, which must have loomed large before her, the day she first came to Waterford.*

*Her feet touched our streets, even as the blood of our ancestors stained them. She was a frightened, beautiful princess, promised, as part of a military alliance, to a man old enough to be her father. The story runs like this.*

In and around the years 1157 and 1167 there was a king named Dermot MacMurrough Kavanagh, ruling the kingdom of Leinster. He was a strong and ambitious king and he dearly wanted to be made king of all Ireland. At that time there were many small or petty kings but the four provinces of Ulster, Munster, Leinster and Connaught had greater kings and ruling over the whole lot of them was Ruairi O Connor – the High King.

The Brehon Laws existed then and there was a law covering every circumstance that could possibly arise in any human relationship.

For a king to have several wives was not uncommon, for didn't it mean that the people of their clan would have to help him in times of difficulty. But it was not just that, there were laws which governed how much 'honour price' must be paid to the first wife or '*ceit muintir*', when he brought in a second wife and so on. Then everyone settled down and the women got on with their lives, quietly ruling their roost, or sometimes not so quietly. But the system worked.

Well it happened that while Dermot was young he had a close friendship with a beautiful girl called Dervogilla. Now Dervogilla came from the Maolachlann clan and they were close allies always of the MacMurrough Kavanaghs, indeed her own brother fought alongside Dermot in most of his battles.

It was the practice at that time for kings to make alliances of political necessity, which usually meant marrying off their sons or daughters into suitable strong kingdoms. Dermot was no different from any other king in this – he had made a marriage with Mor O Toole so as to have strong connections with her clan, and a little while later to Sive O Faolain from a small kingdom, which controlled a section of land between himself and the O Tooles. He was paving his way to High Kingship, he thought.

Well, Dermot was not an easy neighbour for any king and there were often skirmishes between them but it was not until Dermot decided to rescue his old friend Dervogilla Maolachlann from an unhappy marriage to Tiernan O Rourke that his troubles really began.

Now according to the Annals of the Four Masters and other historical records, Dermot was fully to blame, but I am not inclined to believe them, nor indeed are many other modern historians. It was easy for the Church to make Dermot the villain. He was foolish, in a lot of his ways, thinking he was above the law. Sure, didn't he cause the Abbess of Kildare to be raped so that he could put one of his own relatives into power there instead of her? The Abbess had rule over the monks as well as the sisters at that time, so it was a powerful position.

Well, to get back to my story. It appears that Dervogilla had made arrangements with Dermot and her brother that they should spirit her away from her unhappy marriage to Tiernan O Rourke. She was party to the plan, for don't those same records tell us that she had all her goods and chattels ready and waiting for them, when they came in the dead of night and took her back to Leinster.

Now it is also recorded that she cried out for help as she was taken away, but why wouldn't she? If things went wrong she needed a way back. If she had to come back, through whatever cause, she could always claim she was kidnapped. But the fact is that she went to Leinster and spent almost two years living with Dermot, having paid 'honour price' to his first wife Mor, and his second wife Sive, and the three women were very fond of one another, apparently.

Now Tiernan O Rourke was not idle while these years were passing, and in fact all the religious men of power turned against Dermot, so he had more trouble on his hands than he could handle. His two sons, Eanna and Conor, were taken as hostages to ensure his good behaviour, by the High King, and Dermot was in serious trouble because he refused to pay an 'honour price' to O Rourke for the taking of his wife. Had he paid that he might indeed have become the High King, but he didn't and war raged up and down the borders of Leinster.

It was only when his lovely son Eanna, who would have ruled after him, was sent home to him blinded that Dermot realised his mistake. A man with any imperfection, especially of the physical nature, could not rule a clan. But Dermot would not give back Dervogilla and it was only when his kingdom was finally being overrun and the head of his son Conor was sent to him that he gave in. Dervogilla had to go back to O Rourke and Dermot had to flee to Wales, but he took his daughter Aoife and her female servants with him.

Between the two of us, I don't think that going back to her husband lasted long either, for it is said that she entered Mellifont Abbey, shortly after, God help her. She was probably very glad to do that. I wasn't there so I don't know, but by the sound of things he was a terrible man.

The women of Dermot were left behind to take care of things, with his half brother, Murrough, who helped to quiet things down. It was Dermot's intention to ask for help from King Henry II but that king was busy fighting in France and it was almost a year later that Dermot finally caught up with him at Aquitaine. Things didn't really favour Dermot at that meeting, but he did get a letter from the king to take to an out-of-favour earl back in Wales.

He hurried back to Wales and together with Aoife, journeyed to meet Richard de Clare, Earl of Pembroke, otherwise known as Strongbow. No one else would help them. They were all afraid of their own king Henry and watching their own positions. It was common practice then for mercenaries to be hired by Irish kings to fight in Ireland and in turn Welsh kings hired Irish mercenaries. There was nothing new in this seeking aid from across the sea.

Well anyway, Strongbow turned out to be a man as old as Aoife's father, but Dermot promised Strongbow that, if he would help, he could not only marry his lovely daughter Aoife but he could have the kingdom of Leinster, on his death, also. Now that was not his to give, but either Strongbow knew and took the chance, or he didn't know and badly wanted the alliance.

When the lovely Aoife saw this old man and heard her father negotiating, she was mortified. How could her father do this to her, and worse still how could he belittle himself in this way? Strongbow met her eye more than once and even went as far as offering her wine himself. She trembled as their hands touched, when he steadied the goblet, but lifting her dark eyes to the grey of his she saw understanding and sympathy. This shook her more than anything else. Later, when her father was well in his cups, Strongbow sent his women to her, to show her to her rooms.

The deal done, Dermot returned to Ireland in the early summer of 1167, on the pretence that he was going to incarcerate himself in the Abbey in Ferns with the monks. That was common enough in those times, when men wanted to duck out of their duties. Now that was an easy thing for Dermot to announce, for who knew which monk came and went, from there, under a cowl.

Mor welcomed home her daughter and she and Sive listened to all she had to tell them about the man Strongbow and the proposals her father had made. Aoife described Strongbow as being very tall, with a nice face and freckles, and his eyes were grey, but he was very old. Worst of all had been the promises her father had made. Mor shook her head and laughed. Dermot was trying it on with the man, she said. He probably intended to kill him once he had regained the kingdom of Leinster. She knew her man well.

Aoife knew she should be happy about this but there was something in her that went against it. She took to riding out to the cliff tops, facing Wales, and watching to see if the ships bearing Strongbow might come. More often than not, the wind was in the wrong direction. The poor child had a path of her own worn along the headland before long.

Sometimes she would sit with the women and they would tell her how she might please her husband, when he finally came, for they were sure it would not be long now, and they used their skills with needle and loom to make the necessary bridal wear.

Often and often, Aoife began to wonder if Strongbow was going to come at all, and this would change her mood. Sometimes, she was the proud princess going to do her duty, and other times, she was doubtful, thinking that maybe he did not desire her. It was three years later, in 1170, when her husband-to-be finally came, in the month of August. When the ships were sighted, passing along the coast, it was only then Dermot came out from under his monks cowl. Then he rallied his women and men.

Mor and Sive prepared Aoife, whispering advice and laughing, sometimes sad and sometimes joyful.

A messenger came from Strongbow, who had landed at Passage East, in Co. Waterford, and had gone swiftly up to attack that city, without waiting for Dermot. Dermot must have been greatly annoyed but he had made promises and now he must keep them.

That grand Viking city of Waterford, or Vaderfiord, as they had named it, had stood firm, at first, against this attack until Strongbow's man, Raymond le Gros, had discovered a little, lean-to house on the outside of the city wall, by the river. He had sent in men to knock down this house and as it fell away into the river, a big chunk of the city wall fell with it. Then it was an easy matter to flood into the little hilly streets of Waterford, bringing blood and slaughter.

Aoife rode with her father and his men. They could see the smoke and hear the sounds of battle, even before they reached the banks of the River Suir. The only building which stood out strong in the smoke-filled air was the tower that was called Reginald's Tower.

It stood down close on the bank of the river, and so it still stands there this very day. Everything else was shrouded in smoke. Seagulls, rooks and ravens circled over the devastation. Ships burned in the harbour. Screams and cries of terror echoed intermittently on the air. Strongbow had descended on that city with little pity.

It is said that Dermot and his wedding party crossed the river, wading through the dead and dying, while Strongbow and the Normans still fought and pillaged. That may be so, but they probably crossed the river near Passage East, and came in along the road that runs up beside the river from Passage. We have no way of knowing.

There, Dermot presented his daughter, as promised, to his new ally, Strongbow, and they were married. She, according to that pompous man Geraldus Cambrensis, 'was radiantly beautiful', and why wouldn't she be, all young girls are beautiful, but the *cratur* must have had terror in her heart that day. Maybe her father had regrets, but maybe not. Waterford had fallen to his new son-in-law and Dermot was back on his feet again.

Now things did not work out as Dermot expected. Aoife seems to have loved Strongbow and they had a good life. She never attempted to 'repudiate' him, as she could easily have done under the Brehon Laws. We should never have let those laws go, we could do with them badly now.

Aoife filled the role of advisor to her husband. She knew the lie of the land and what would work in the way of alliances. They spent time, always battle ready, in Waterford, Wexford and Dublin, if the old tales are to be believed.

She prevented her father from trying to kill him, and she and Strongbow had one daughter, Isabelle, who, in turn, married William le Mareschal, Earl Marshal of Ireland. They had many sons and daughters and they all made good political marriages. One of these marriages, it is reported, resulted in the lineage which leads down to the present-day Queen of England, Her Majesty Queen Elizabeth II. You never know what way your children will turn out in the end.

In Waterford, we like to think of Aoife as one of our own, after all wasn't she married in our city, and she only a young princess. She was strong and brave and must have been glad to get away from her father and his plotting and planning. She lived for many years after Strongbow and although there is a tomb in Christ Church in Dublin, where it is said Strongbow is buried, other sources claim that he is buried in the churchyard in Ferns, in Co. Wexford. My belief is that there are as many endings to their story as there are scribes who write about it.

## Two

# PETTICOAT LOOSE

When I was a little girl, growing up in the 1950s and '60s, it was often and often that I would hear mention of Petticoat Loose. Sometimes a girl would be told to 'tidy herself up' and not go around like Petticoat Loose. Over the years, my own parents and visiting neighbours might compare a young woman who was not conducting herself as they thought she should to Petticoat Loose or as the local saying went 'She was a right streel, like Petticoat Loose'.

The story of Petticoat Loose was only told when the little ones had gone to bed. So, for a long time, I did not get the rights of it. However, we had a lovely neighbour named Denny Maher. He had been a friend to my parents since childhood and it was from him I finally heard the tale, as he knew it.

I was working in Tramore, at the time, and telling Denny how I used to cycle from there to my home, some twelve miles distant. Denny drew in a sharp breath and said that I was a foolish girl to be on that road, between Waterford and Tramore, on a dark night. I made light of it, thinking he was just joking me but he wasn't. 'Did you never hear about Petticoat Loose being on that road?' says he.

'Ah go away now Denny', says I.

Before many minutes were out, however, I knew more than I wanted to know about that stretch of road, halfway between Waterford and Tramore. There is a part along there where a little bridge turns off, and it was near this place that the dreaded Petticoat Loose was often seen. What she was doing there the Lord only knows, but I believe her spirit roamed over the whole of Co. Waterford. Honest to God, wouldn't it make you wonder about the after life, the carry-on of some ghosts.

Her name was, according to Denny, Mary Hannigan and she came from the townland of Colligan, outside Dungarvan. She was a fine lump of a woman, bless her, and she could turn her hand to any work on the farm where she grew up. Better than two men, 'twas said. Most of all she loved to dance, and she was a great dancer; not every big woman is, but Mary Hannigan had music in her very bones and she attended every house dance and gathering in the surrounding areas.

Well it is through the dancing that she got her name, Petticoat Loose. It was the fashion then for women and girls to wear layers of clothing, not like now, God help us. One of the staple garments was the petticoat, which could be like an under skirt or indeed a full slip-like garment. Well, for the dancing it appears that a flouncy underskirt was the petticoat in question and Mary swirled around the floor, skirts flying and feet tapping, like none other until disaster struck. Didn't the petticoat come loose, and came away down around her ankles. Sure she must have been mortified with embarrassment, the *cratur*, which was made worse by the titters and giggles of those present.

Something was said which aggravated Mary, to the point that she let fly with a fist and a bit of a tussle ensued. Ever after she was called Petticoat Loose, and there was no getting away from a name put on you, in a country place, for a thing like that.

Despite the name there were many who wished to marry her, but she was not inclined to take up with any of them. The one who finally won her hand was the son of a neighbouring farmer. He too was, by all accounts, a fine strapping lad. There must be something in the air around Colligan.

They were married and settled down together without too much fuss or bother, in the beginning, but among the other suitors who had chased after the single Petticoat Loose, there was another man who believed she should have married him instead.

They say that he was a hedge school master, who came and went in the area. He was daft about her and they must have kept up their relationship when they could manage it.

Well things were not going too well on the farm and there were often complaints from people who got milk from them, that it was watered down, and that it had a blueish hue to it.

There came an evening when Mary Hannigan and a servant girl were milking the cows and on the evening air came the sound of a man calling out in grave distress and a sudden cry. The serving girl leapt up to run and see but was knocked flat by a blow from the milking stool thrown by Mary Hannigan. The girl said after that she got a terrible fright and hurt bad, her poor head spinning. She was afraid for her life. Petticoat Loose stood over her as she lay, stunned, in the milking parlour. She told her to get back to the milking and mind her own business.

Sure the little girl was afraid to do anything but what she was told. She had her own thoughts on the matter and it came as no surprise to her to find that farmer Whelan was nowhere to be found in the days that came after.

When people asked Petticoat Loose where her husband was she replied that he had gone away often before and he would come back some time. No more than that would she say.

In a small rural community, talk will always run away with itself and in no time at all it was put about that she had enlisted the help of her lover, the hedge schoolmaster, to kill her husband and dispose of his body. Those who used to work on the farm drifted away from her, she was so contrary, and she did little or no dancing now, only drinking. 'Bless us and save us', they said, 'she would drink like a fish'. Some said she was really a witch and in those times people were ready to believe anything. Some still do to this very day. Well, whether Petticoat Loose was a witch or not, it was her fondness for the drink that finally did for her.

She was in the habit of challenging the men to drinking contests and it was during one of these awful sessions that, after consuming a gallon of beer, she suddenly fell over, stone dead.

It was normal then, and indeed now, to call a priest or some member of the clergy to attend at a sudden death, but no one called either priest or deacon to come, to officiate over the remains of Petticoat Loose. Not even for her burial did a religious attend. They buried her without benefit of Church or people. I often wondered about that. Was her death natural?

Well, life in the area settled down into normal humdrum activities and all was well for about seven years. Now the importance of seven in country superstitions is well known. Sure don't we still hear about men getting the seven-year itch?

It happened this way. There was a house dance in the locality and as we all know, at that time there were no inside loos, only a little lean-to houseen at the side of the barn. This is where the men would dash out to when the need arose. Well it appears that around twelve o'clock at night one of the young bucks went out to, as they say, make water. He was barely gone out when he came back in, and his face like chalk and the life nearly gone out of him.

'She is out there', he said, 'Petticoat Loose is out in the yard'. Sure they all burst out laughing at him and gave him a stiff whiskey. Soon after that another young fellow went out, on the same errand, and he too came bolting back in and the whites of his eyes showing, like a startled horse.

'She is out there', he said, and this time no one laughed. They were all afraid, you see, afraid to go out into that dark night in case they too might see the spectre of Petticoat Loose. So they stayed where they were until daylight came. But the rumours went out and after that there were many sightings of Petticoat Loose, in and around the county.

Some of the sightings were more frightening than others, and many said that if you were travelling alone at night then she would stop you and beg a lift. Because she always appeared as a frightened woman, most people would agree to give her a lift and invite her to sit up on the pony's trap. (They had no motor cars in those times, only horse or pony and trap, or even ass-drawn traps.) Well, if she sat up on the side of the trap, more often than not the poor animal drawing it would start to falter or not be able to move at all. She would laugh and vanish, leaving both driver and animal spooked so much that they would never be right again.

One night she stopped a man on the Tramore road, near that little bridge, and asked him for a lift. Thinking nothing of it he said 'Surely, let you sit up on the trap.' She did, bless us and save us, and no sooner had she rested on it than the poor horse began to falter.

The man said, 'I don't know what ails him at all', and she laughed a horrible laugh. 'Look at me', says she. 'This arm weighs a ton', and she plonked her right arm heavily on the trap. The animal struggled to keep going. 'Now look at this arm', said she holding up her left arm. 'This too weighs a ton.' The poor driver was wide eyed with fear now and the trap was groaning and creaking. 'No more,' he cried out. But she said, 'Look at this leg, it weighs a ton'.

The trap came to a standstill and, speechless with terror, the driver watched as she raised her second leg and placed it into the trap. 'This

leg weighs a ton also,' said she. And lastly she clasped her hands on her belly and said 'and this too weighs a ton'. At that the trap broke into smithereens and the man fell in a dead faint. It was the horse running, with the ruined trap behind him, that raised the alarm.

Well after that not many people went on the roads of Co. Waterford, alone at night. They say that her ghost became so troublesome that in the end the people begged the priests for help. Now whether it is true or not, there was a priest, a Fr Meaney, 'tis said, in the parish of Kilrossanty and Fews, did you ever hear of it? Well in every diocese there is one priest who is supposed to do exorcisms and banishments and the like, and this priest was the one to tackle the ghost of Petticoat Loose.

It seems that he went out looking for her, with some learned and brave men, and they carrying all sorts of protections, like holy water, hazel rods, rosary beads, rush crosses and the like. The holy priest called out for Petticoat Loose to show herself and she duly did. Just to be on the safe side he called to her to say who she was. It would be terrible if he made a mistake, bless us and save us, but she answered that she was indeed the ghost of Petticoat Loose.

They were very frightened, for her aspect was terrifying. But the priest was not afraid and so he began the banishment, and he told her he was banishing her to the bottom of Baylough up in the Knockmealdown Mountains, a place apparently known to himself and herself, and it not at all far from Colligan, the place where she was born. He banished her there under the stricture that she could not leave that place until she made a *sugán* or rope from the sand she found on the bottom. He said other words too, in Latin, and when he was finished she was gone.

The men with him clapped him on the back and said he was a powerful man altogether. The priest said, 'It wasn't me but the words, but now I feel I have used up all my strength.' By the time two more weeks had passed, he too was gone to his Maker.

My storyteller, Denny, let the silence last a few minutes, breathing in soft shooing sounds. Then shaking his head he said, 'Wasn't it a terrible thing entirely to happen so near our own place. Now don't be going that road on your own, in the dark, now pet. Are you listening to me?'

I was – and I didn't.

## Three

# THE THREE SISTERS —
# THE RIVER GODDESSES

*This story is based on old mythology but according to the Annals of Leinster it is not necessarily correct in detail. Sure, as my mother, God rest her would say, 'What did they know?'*

*It is my own belief that this story was told in the following manner for a different reason i.e. earth and nature worship. You will see why I think this.*

In the very early years of settlement, by different peoples, this country of Ireland had a very different way of working. People were very tribal and little communities had their own traditions and ways of doing things. Not least of these was the act of worship. Man has always believed in a power or powers greater than themselves. So there were sun worshippers, nature worship and many other different paths followed.

Most places had sacred sites and followed the Gods or Goddesses of that place. They had sacred oak groves, sacred wells and rivers and high places. These places of worship and respect were everywhere. They needed all these places for their day-to-day living. They believed in their own dependence on the good will of these deities, for their own health and wealth and that of their animals and land. Well, we all understand now that to believe in something gives it power and so it did then.

I do not recall when I first heard this story but it was a long time ago and for such a simple story, set so long ago, it has often caused people to get annoyed because they had heard it differently. However, here is my own memory of the story and *má ta breag ann ní mise a cum na a ceap é* (this is my story and if there is a lie in it, it was not I who first told or thought of it).

Look back with me, now, and see how then and now, in the south-east of the country, three rivers flowed through different landscapes until they came together in a great surge before going out to join the sea in one great rush. They meet the sea at the place we call Dunmore East. They are now called The Suir, The Nore and The Barrow and are known far and wide as The Three Sisters.

Long ago they had other names and each one had a resident Goddess. These Goddesses were sisters, and were called Eiru, Banba and Fodhla. Each Goddess had her own worshippers and followers in their own regions, and accepted due reverences from them. In return, they saw to it that the lands were never flooded, more than their people could cope with. Also they provided fish, fowl and tubers of various riverbank reeds and plants. They were a highway, a means of transport, for the routine living of all who called on them. Sure there were no roads then, only tracks, so travel on the rivers was very widely used. Their banks were lush and fertile and great stands of forests spread out between them.

Now I told you already, that they were three sisters and as you probably know, sisters sometimes disagree. Eiru, Banba and Fodhla were no different, even though they were Goddesses. In fact, they were probably much more dangerous. It seems that they were often in dispute as to which one of them was the greatest, wisest, most beautiful, had the most followers, you know how these things go.

Being very busy in their own ways they took little or no interest in the puny wars and disagreements of mortals until it became apparent that they were losing followers. A war was being waged between the resident peoples, called the Tuatha de Dannan and an invading force known as the Milesians. The three sisters took this personally and decided to go and take a look at what was happening.

Together they stood up on the headland and were astonished to see the huge spread of the invading fleet, stretching out along the coast. They were surprised also to note that among the invaders there were some who had mystical powers. Eiru, Banba and Fodhla

had led a sheltered existence and never gave much thought to the powers others might master. As they watched the attempts being made by the invaders to land and secure a toehold on the shore, they understood that the Tuatha de Dannan were not going to win this battle. Once this happened, this new mystical power might very well overthrow their little territories. It was not their habit to interfere with the wars of men, but they felt something must be done to safeguard their own sanctuary and that of their followers.

By means available to Goddesses, they were able to find out that the most powerful druid among the invading forces was one called Amergin. Every time the ships were driven back by the storm winds, sent by the Tuatha de Dannan, Amergin rallied the ships and again and again they came against the shore. Being the sons of Mil, the Milesians were never going to give up. The three sisters gathered together fearfully and decided that something had to be done.

Together they waited until the druids of the Tuatha de Dannan were exhausted and their people withdrew from the fight. Then, together, they went to the shore and watched Amergin as he came forward, alone in a small craft. He showed no fear and they drew on all the power within them as he advanced. When he set foot on the sandy beach, a shiver of fear coursed through them. Here was power indeed. As he approached them Eiru stepped forward and asked what business he had landing here. His answer was simple. 'We can not go back, we bring our women and children. Our wish is to settle here in peace.'

'You have killed our followers, we do not want you here', said Eiru. She looked back at her sisters and they nodded agreement.

Amergin tried a different way. 'Let us walk a little way and we can discuss this problem. I am weary from being tossed about on the waves.'

Eiru walked with him. They talked for a time and then Amergin made his best offer. 'My people will replace the followers you have lost and we will call this land in your name, if you agree to let us come here peacefully.'

Eiru thought about it for a little and saw no reason to say no. She was secretly delighted that she had been the one to speak with Amergin first. She would be known forever by his followers.

'It pleases me but I must ask my sisters,' she said.

Amergin was wiser than he looked, so he said, immediately. 'I do not wish to cause any upset between you and your sisters so perhaps it would be best if I spoke to each one separately, then they can not blame you for making the decision.'

Eiru was grateful, for she did not see her sisters agreeing to this very easily. 'It shall be so', she said regally and walked tall as she went up the beach beside Amergin.

Banba next walked with Amergin and again he put the proposal to her but this time he offered to replace her followers with his own people and that he would call the country in the name of Banba.

Banba looked out at the multitude of people still waiting to land and thought how she would have more followers than anyone and she too nodded her agreement.

Last of all Fodhla walked the golden sands with Amergin. She too came to an agreement with him except that he would have his people become her followers and would call the land in the name of Fodhla.

The sisters all secretly rejoiced that they had outwitted the others, each one believing that their name would be the one which had all these new followers and that they would have the whole land named for them. They withdrew to their respective territories of The Suir, The Nore and The Barrow to await developments.

Well, Amergin had not made any promise he could not keep. As his people came to land in their thousands, he divided them into three groups. The first group he instructed that they should settle around the land of the River Suir and that they would call this country Eiru. The second group he sent to the area around the River Nore and said they must call this country Banba. The last group were, of course, sent to the area around the River Barrow and they were to call this country Fodhla. So it was.

Whether the three sisters were angry or not, I can not tell you. But as time went by and the seasons turned the new invaders settled, worshiped the local Gods and Goddesses, and revered the sacred places. Time is the Great Changer so slowly people began to forget the old ways and the only sure thing that now remains, is the fact that Ireland is still referred to in writings and memory as Éire, Banba and Fodhla.

The River Suir rises in the Silvermine Mountains, in Tipperary. It floods down past the towns of Thurles, Holycross, Cahir, Clonmel, Carrick-on-Suir and the City of Waterford, before joining with its sister rivers near Cheekpoint. Then they race away together to meet the sea. (The pet name for the Suir in Waterford is The Quay River). The Suir is tidal up past Carrick-on-Suir, where it turns and sometimes causes flooding.

The Nore rises on the eastern slopes of the Devil's Bit Mountain in North Tipperary. It takes a roundabout path through Durrow in Co. Laois and then on through Kilkenny, Thomastown and Inistioge, where it becomes tidal. It joins with the River Barrow above New Ross and together they flow on to join the Suir below the Barrow Bridge near Cheekpoint.

The Barrow is the longest and most prominent of the three rivers. It rises on the northern end of the Slieve Bloom Mountains in Co. Laois. It passes through Portarlington, Athy, Carlow, Graiguemanagh and New Ross. The Barrow is tidal up as far as St Mullins.

# Four

# Famine Stories

*These two little stories relate to the time of the famine, when poor people were in a terrible state with the hunger. They are part of a series of stories given to me by the late Denny Maher, of the Cloone Road, God be good to him.*

## The Sacred Cow

'Did your father ever tell you the story of the Sacred Cow?' Denny liked to start with a question always, in case you knew it and he was wasting your time. At the shake of my head he would continue, with great enthusiasm.

'Well it was like this Pet, in famine times terrible things happened. You know about the famine now don't you? People were starving and they were so desperate that they were even trying to eat the grass on the side of the road, bless us and save us all. Sure they didn't know that the animals that eat grass have more than one stomach, you see. We weren't made to eat grass at all so the poor creatures would be found dead in a short while and the green of the grass still around their poor wasted mouths.

'It was a terrible time indeed and some people gave up altogether, in despair, don't you see, while others hoped and prayed and clung on desperately, trying to save themselves and their little children. Ah, yes the poor little children, God save us all.

'The worst part of all was that there was grain and food being shipped out of that port down there by the British, while the people were dying of hunger. They never liked us, you know. They wanted the land but not the people.

'Well to get back to my story, there were a few good souls who had pity on the hungry and starving around here. I worked one time as a farmer's labourer, sure we all did when we were young, and there was many a strange thing you learned as you went from one farmer to another. On one farm, I am not sure now of where exactly it was, but there was in the corner of a field near the road, a great big iron pot which they said was used as a famine soup pot.

'Those who could, would gather up what ever food they were able, be it vegetables or a bit of meat and anything that was edible, at all, and it was thrown into this mighty big iron pot and cooked up. Sure they said you could get the smell of the cooking for miles around. Anyone who was strong enough to get to where it was cooking would be sure of a hot meal. It would be enough to keep them going for another day, the poor hungry people. It was to be expected then that some of them would hang on around the area where the soup pot was set up. Sure you would do it yourself, wouldn't you? It was a terrible time, don't you see.

'They were cold and hungry all the time and sometimes there would be no soup in the pot so people prayed and prayed. Then, in this very place where I am telling you about, not far from the Suir River, didn't the strangest thing happen.

'Out of the mists, on a desperately cold evening, came a fine healthy cow and she lowing gently. She just came out and stood among them and they huddled in weakness and hunger. At first they were afraid that they were dreaming again. They often dreamed of having food and why wouldn't they?

'When they realised that she was a real, healthy animal, they were afraid that it was a trick by the landowner and that they would all be killed if they touched her but hunger is a terrible thing, especially when children are crying. So the minute the first one went to the cow they all followed and by the time darkness fell every blessed one of them had a full belly. There is nothing like warm milk, fresh from a cow, I tell you.

'The people thanked God and fell asleep. The Sacred Cow went back into the mists but in the morning she came back again. Well, it went on like that for a while and they tried to keep quiet about the fact that they were getting this milk but people talk and people have relatives, and in no time at all there were twice as many people waiting each morning and evening for the Sacred Cow to give milk.

'The thing they should have done Pet, was to stay a little while and drink enough milk to get strong and then to move on. They should have tried to find food or work somewhere else, but they were getting it too handy, you see. Now instead of just a few poor hungry people waiting for the Sacred Milk, there were hundreds and hundreds waiting for her to come out of the mists and there

was pushing and shoving and crying and moaning as they tried to get a turn at milking her.

'Some even went so far as to talk about putting a halter around her and keeping her in the one spot but sure she needed to graze in heavenly pastures every night, the bountiful creature. But people can be very cruel and so instead of being grateful they began to take the Sacred Cow for granted. It is a flaw in human nature, child. We can get like that, God help us.

'Well one evening they milked and milked the Sacred Cow and didn't the wonderful creature just fall down dead from all the milking. Bless us and save us all, they didn't know when they had enough and now they had nothing again. They blamed each other, of course, but it was too late. Never again did the Sacred Cow come lowing out of the mists to feed anyone.'

## THE SHOAL OF FISH

'There was another story now, and I don't know if you heard this, but down on the banks of the River Suir, a long time ago now it was, at the time of the great famine.

'The people should have been able to help themselves, you would think, they living beside the river and the sea as they were. But it was never that easy. You forget, you see, that our own people were living under the yoke of the invader. They had little or no rights at all, bless us and save us. If they were caught fishing or even cutting fire wood they could be hanged in a minute. Wasn't that a terrible state of affairs altogether?

'Well Pet, I think that even God can get annoyed sometimes at the cruelties humans inflict on each other. When it seemed that there was little or no hope for poor families, with young children, bless us and save us, and they huddled in little makeshift huts down near the river, didn't God send to them a miracle.

'It was down near the bend of the river, where the little boats used to go out to meet the big ships. There had been a big storm, for the weather didn't stand still then either Pet, and sometimes people would find bits and pieces washed up on the banks of the river when the rage of the storm was spent. A group of people, and they hungry, were scavenging along the bank. Anything washed up they could claim as their own, you see. Well, they came around the bend of the river and there, flapping and throwing themselves about on the bank were hundreds of fish.

'You can imagine the panic, can't you, Pet. The people sent back word to their families and they gathered and gathered as many fish as they could manage. Sure they had little or nothing to take them back in. Some wise women brought sheets from off the beds and they gathered in the shining, shimmering fish.

'Oh there was feasting that night, I can tell you, and not a thing the landlords could do about it. Anyone who could and knew how salted or smoked some of their miraculous catch but mostly they just shared them out with everyone and anyone. Fish don't keep well, you know.

'It was enough to keep them going for little while and there was always the hope that things would get better tomorrow, God help them all. Ever after they searched and searched up and down the banks, on both sides of the river, but never again did a miraculous shoal of fish offer themselves up to the hungry on the banks of the River Suir.'

## Five

# THE WELL AND THE GOLDEN DRAGON

A young married man and his wife once went out to gather rushes for Lá Féile Bríde (St Brigid's Day). They knew where some fine, strong rushes grew. They were nice, plump rushes and of the very best quality. They had seen them, several times, as they walked through the woods in Ballycahane.

The rushes were to be used for making the St Brigid's Crosses, which are traditionally made to hang behind the doors and ward off danger and sickness. The farmers liked to hang them in the cow houses and barns as well. St Brigid was great for blessing the animals and was also said to be strong protection against fire.

The young married man and his wife talked about the making of the crosses and how many they needed for family and friends. It was a good thing to do together, and the carrying on of the tradition was important to them. It would have to be done smartly now, because it would be dark early. The crosses had to be made and placed outside the door in a basket, for the tradition was that St Brigid would pass by each house after dark and bless the crosses and ribbons in the basket. The ribbons were used to prevent headaches and, since long ago, every household had a blessed ribbon which would be bound around the head to cure a headache.

As they drew near the place they were seeking, the evening was quiet and still. St Brigid's Eve is the last day of January and it can be cold and even snowy, at times. The clumps of rushes were there in all their glory. The longest and finest rushes they had ever seen. The only problem was that they were sited beyond a deep pool of water. They stood on the pathway, for a minute or two, trying to figure out how to reach them. Not a leaf stirred and only the shrill call of the blackbird echoed through the valley.

The woman shivered. The blackbird is a bird of the threshold between this world and the next, and she knew this. It was getting late so she hurried her husband. He took a flying leap and landed on a solid raised grass tuft near the rushes. He bent and with a quick slicing movement he cut through a bunch of the rushes. The blackbird shrilled again and the woman suddenly felt very uneasy. 'Come back here quick', she called. He looked up, startled, but seeing her face, made the jump and landed beside her.

'What is it?' He asked but she didn't answer him, only grabbed his arm and began to drag him quickly back along the path.

The silence which had hung over the woods was gone. There was a shifting and rustling all around them. Sounds they could not identify, panting and snuffling. As they hurried, along the pathway, so too did the sounds, all around them. To one side it seemed that something huge and lumbering was keeping pace with them. In the end, out of breath and very frightened they stopped. Whatever it was, they did not want to have it follow them home.

The woman called out. 'We meant no harm. We only came for the rushes for Lá Féile Bhríde. Naomh Bhríde, the holy woman, Brigit. We meant no harm.'

The rustling and movement all around them stopped. All that they could hear now was their own rapid breathing and something like a sigh. A deep, ancient sounding, sigh. It seemed to come from the very earth itself. It was then that the woman saw them. On the path ahead stood a strong healthy fox, to the right-hand side of it stood a tall brown bear and on the left-hand side, half lost in the trees, stood a great golden dragon.

'We are the guardians of the sacred place'. The voice was deep and purring. The dragon's eyes glowed green and gold. 'You may not take anything from there. But we know of Brigit. In her name we allow you to leave in peace.'

The woman's voice came in a whisper. 'We can not undo what we have done. We are sorry. We will make an offering instead if that is acceptable.'

There was a long silence and then, even as she watched the guardians of that sacred place, shimmered and withdrew.

She scrabbled in her pocket and took out a precious stone, which she always carried, and urgently asked her husband for a silver coin. Together they went back to the place from whence they had cut the rushes and as the sun slanted through the trees, making the water sparkle, they dropped in to it the precious stone and the silver coin. A deep sigh seemed to breathe through that quiet clearing and from far off they heard the blackbird trill a different note.

Together they walked from the water and the trees and no word passed between them. The making of the crosses took place in silence also and it was only when the rush crosses were placed safely in the basket outside the door that they felt able to speak about what had happened.

In the years that followed they often visited that holy site and dropped offerings in the water. Sometimes they felt the presence of others and once a wolf made his appearance as they stood in silent communion.

Blessings were sought and given and once on a winter's evening, when snowflakes floated softly down, the man sang a great song of praise that thrilled and echoed through the valley and the world stopped to listen.

Imbolc is celebrated at the same time as St Brigid's Day. It celebrates the coming of spring and is a time of preparation for the tilling and sowing. In olden times it was Brigit, daughter of the Father God, Dagda, who was invoked for the blessings on crops and animals. Brigit is honoured in many lands but in Ireland we claim her as our own even though, it appears that there have been many holy women called Brigit or Brigid, who have succeeded her down to Christian times. What do we know? Anything is possible. So, '*Ar eagla na heagla*' (for fear of the fear) or just in case, we still invoke the blessing of our present-day St Brigid.

The tradition of making St Brigid's Crosses is strong in Co. Waterford. Many schools are called after the saint and it is usual for schools, especially country schools, to teach the children how to make the Cros Bhríde. There is a St Brigid's Well – *Tobar Bhríde* located in Dungarvan. It is the well from which the Distillery, known once as St Brigid's Well Distillery, draws its water.

In recent times a lovely bronze sculpture of a child lying on a granite rock who appears to be trying to reach into a rain-filled pool, where there is a stone carved with a Cros Bhríde, has been set near St Brigid's Well Housing Development. The piece, called *Tobar Bhríde*, is by Cliodhna Cussen.

## Six

# HOW COXTOWN·
# WAS NAMED

A sea captain anchored his boat in a small cove on the Co. Waterford coast and, as he paced the deck at night, he noticed a ball of fire descending slowly from the sky. Gradually, it came lower and lower until it touched a house situated some distance inland. While he was expecting the house to burst into flames at any moment, a cock crowed and the ball of fire disappeared instantly. The next night, exactly the same thing happened, just as the ball of flames was about to touch the house the cock crowed and again the ball of fire disappeared.

This performance was repeated a further two nights in succession until the captain became extremely desirous of possessing the cock.

The following day he went into Dunmore and walked up the hill until he approached the house where the cock was and talked to the owner of the house. On meeting the owner the captain made small talk about the weather, not wanting the owner to see how keen he was to get the cock. After a while the talk turned to the topic of noise and the owner said that he had a cock that kept waking him at night with its crowing and he wanted to get rid of him as he had not had a good night's sleep in years. The captain offered the owner a silver shilling for the cock and took it with him back to the boat

The next night he set himself to watch the house as usual and the ball of fire descended on the house which was now without its protector and it burst into flames and burned to the ground. The following evening the captain set sail and as midnight approached, a ball of fire came out of the sky and was about to engulf the boat in flames when the cock crowed and the ball fell into the water. The story has it that the area was for ever after called 'Coileach' a cock, now called Coxtown.

*This story was given to me by Noel McDonagh from Dunmore East in Co. Waterford.*

## Seven

# IOMPAR Á MHÁLA —
# THE BAG CARRIER

There's an old fence in the parish of Dunhill, a boundary between three townlands – Dunhill, Ballyphilip and the High Place of the River. There is a stream running by the side of it, and there is terrible damage when this stream floods. It was during a flood that the 'Bag Carrier' – *Iompar á Mhála* – was drowned. His ghost used to be seen there at night, and fear prevented anyone from travelling there after nightfall.

Now, there was a farmer in the area, and a *scoláire bocht* – a poor student – would come to his house at various times to teach his children. He used to come to the house by crossing the haunted river. One night the farmer bet the poor student a pound that he would not go back across that river. 'It's a bet,' said the student.

It was a beautiful moonlit night. Down went the poor student to the fence of the three boundaries, while the farmer and his sons watched from afar. The student crossed the river, but who was standing on a stone in front of him but the Bag Carrier. The farmer and his sons saw the spirit and off they took as fast as their legs could move the earth underneath them.

'*In ainm Dé,*' said the student to the Carrier, '*cad tá tú ag déanamh annso?*'

'It is a long time I'm here,' said the spirit, 'and no one has ever had the courage to speak to me, but there's an end to the penance. Come with me now and I'll show you something that will do you good.'

The Carrier brought him to a stile in the fence. Up they went onto the path at the top of the fence and in they went to Ballyphilip hill.

'Put a stick in there,' said the Carrier to him and his finger pointing at a certain sod on the side of the hill. 'Dig that place and you'll find a crock of gold. But you don't need to spend any of it on me because I'm damned. When I was drowning and the stone went from under my foot, what I said was "*M'anam ag an diabhal*" [my soul to the Devil] instead of "*M'anam ón diabhal*" [save my soul from the Devil] that's a mistake I made and I'm paying for it dearly.'

That same night the student got a pick and a shovel and started to dig where he was shown. And sure enough the crock of gold was there. The following day, he went to the parish priest in Dunhill and asked him to say Mass, on a certain Sunday, for the soul of the Bag Carrier. After that he went around to every priest in the area and gave them money for the same cause. All the Masses were to be said on the same Sunday. He stayed going around from priest to priest until all the money was spent.

When that was done, he made his way back home. It was a stormy night and he was crossing the path where there is now a bridge on the road between Fenor and Ballyadam, but there was no bridge there that time, only a path. Going over the path, what did he see under the fence but a man and a poor appearance on him.

'*In ainm Dé*,' said the *scoláire bocht*, 'what brought you out on such a night?'

'Six children I've left at home behind me,' said the man, 'and they shouting with the hunger. I could get no patience in listening to them. I had to go and see if I could get them something to eat some way or another.'

'I only have one sovereign left,' said the student. 'Here, you take it, and say a prayer for the man who drowned in the stream at the fence of the three boundaries. And another thing, there will be Mass said for him in every church in the diocese tomorrow morning.'

The poor man went down on his knees in the water on the path and said a prayer to God for the dead.

Now there was an old thatched church in Fenor at that time, situated where Mrs Cheasty has the little wood today. When the priest turned to the congregation at the final prayer, he announced that

Mass that morning was for the soul of the Bag Carrier. While he was talking, a white crow flew in the door and up on the altar he went.

'Are you the soul of the Bag Carrier?' asked the priest.

'I am,' said the white crow.

'Was it myself that freed you?' asked the priest.

'It was not,' said the crow.

'Then who was it freed you?' asked the priest.

'It was the man that went down on his knees in the water on the path in Fenor last night,' said the crow. 'From his heart came the prayer that saved me.'

*From a story in the collection of the Folklore Department of University College, Dublin. It was written in Irish by Maurice Lacy, school teacher, Fenor, who had heard it from Martin Farrell of Fenor. Máiréad Murphy of Dunhill translated it for folklorist Julian Walton. This story was further passed on to me for this collection by Julian.*

# Eight

# Mrs Rogers' Dream Comes True

Way back in the 1780s there lived in Portlaw an innkeeper named Rogers and his wife. One night Mrs Rogers had a dream. Two men dressed as sailors arrived at the inn, a tall man and a short man. They had some refreshment, and then went on their way towards Carrick-on-Suir. In her dream she followed them and saw, to her horror, the smaller of the two men strike the taller, stab him as he lay on the ground, rob him, and bury him beside a hedge.

On waking, Mrs Rogers in great agitation told her husband of her dream. Imagine her horror when, later that day, there arrived two men whom she instantly recognised as the two she had seen in her dream. They drank together in apparent friendship and then, despite the Rogers' entreaties that they should stay for the night, continued their journey. Not long afterwards, one of the two men returned to Waterford, alone. His name was Caulfield, a grave man of decent appearance and serious, religious manners. He appeared to have come into some money, for he ordered twelve new shirts, and as he was in a hurry had them made by twelve different seamstresses.

Some time after, news reached Waterford of people in Cork who had expected a friend named Hickey returning via Waterford from the fisheries in Newfoundland, where he had evidently made some

money. He had not turned up. Was it possible that Caulfield and Hickey were the two men in Mrs Rogers's dream?

The obvious way to find out was to walk the road between Portlaw and Carrick until they came to the spot where Mrs Rogers had seen the murder take place. She recognised it instantly, and there, buried beside the hedge, was the body of the unfortunate Hickey.

Caulfield was arrested and put on trial. His defence council did his best to ridicule the evidence provided by the prosecution, but the Rogers remained firm. The judge declared that Providence had directly intervened to secure justice against a murderer, and on receiving sentence Caulfield confessed his guilt.

The news of this extraordinary trial spread far and wide, and there was a constant stream of visitors to the jail to interview the penitent criminal. Caulfield was a handsome man, particularly attentive to his dress, and the ladies sent him various articles of clothing so that he might select the apparel in which he should be executed. He was accompanied to the gallows, which was about a mile outside the town, by a large attendance of respectable people who gathered around it chanting the 51st psalm, in which – we are assured – Mr Caulfield joined with fervent piety.

*Main source: J.E. Walsh,* Ireland Sixty Years Ago *(Dublin, 1847), pp. 115-19. My thanks to Julian Walton for this story.*

Nine

# CURRAGHMORE ESTATE STORIES

## THE CRYSTAL OF CURRAGHMORE

Did you ever hear of the Crystal of Curraghmore? Very few people still recall that it even exists but I came across a reference to it, by accident, and I made enquiries at Curraghmore Estate in Portlaw in Co. Waterford.

The information I had came from a book, written by Lady Wilde – *Ancient Legends of Ireland*, published by Ward & Downey; London, 1888. It was reprinted by O'Gorman Ltd, Galway Ireland in 1971. Page 209 reads as follows:

'Charms by Crystals'
The charms by crystals are of great antiquity in Ireland – a mode of divination, no doubt, brought from the East by the early wandering tribes. Many of these stones have been found throughout the country, and are held in great veneration. They are generally globular, and appear to have been originally set in royal sceptres or sacred shrines. A very ancient crystal globe of this kind, with miraculous curative powers, is still to be seen at Curraghmore, the seat of the Marquis of Waterford, and it is believed to have been brought from

the Holy Land by one of the Le Poers, who had it as a gift from Godfrey de Bouillon. The ball is of rock crystal, a little larger than an orange, and is circled round the middle by a silver band. It is still constantly borrowed by the people to effect cures upon cattle suffering from murrain or other distempers. This is done by placing the ball in a running stream, through which the cattle are driven backwards and forwards many times.

The peasants affirm that the charm never fails in success, and the belief in its miraculous powers is so widespread that people from the most distant parts of Ireland send to Curraghmore to borrow it. Even to this day the faith in its magic power continues unabated, and requests for the loan come from every quarter. The Marquis of Waterford leaves it in the care of his steward, and it is freely loaned to all comers; but to the credit of the people it may be noted, that the magic crystal is always brought back to Curraghmore with the most scrupulous care.*

*Extract from a letter by the Marchioness of Waterford, on the Curraghmore Crystal.

In response to my query, I was assured that, not only did the crystal exist but it was kept in a special glass case, in the home of the present Marquis of Waterford, John Hubert de La Poer Beresford, 8th Marquis of Waterford.

Lord Waterford generously offered to show it to me, even though it was not on public display for tours coming and going to the estate to view the famous Shell House and gardens.

I arrived at the appointed time. The avenue was long and when eventually I came in sight of Curraghmore House it was like something out of an old romantic novel. Two great big arms of long buildings embraced me as I entered the gate. Many workers were busily hurrying in and out of these buildings. The main house stood large and elegant, closing off the far end of this wonderful courtyard. Wide flag steps took me up to the huge black door.

The bell rang somewhere deep inside and a young man came quickly to greet me. He went to inform his lordship of my arrival.

I could hear them come, with quiet talk and the skittering of dogs' paws on the big hall floor.

Lord Waterford was very gracious in his welcome and to my delight he produced the famous crystal out of his jacket pocket and laid it carefully down on top of a timber chest. He placed beside it a small descriptive tag. This, he informed me, contained the information his late mother had left with it.

The crystal is, to my understanding, clear quartz. It is, for all the world, the size of the hopping balls we used to play with against the wall in school, back in the 1950s and '60s. It is larger than a golf ball and not as big as a tennis ball. The silver band around it is not very wide and is tied off like a small cross shape. It is embedded in the crystal and is dark with age, as one would expect.

There is a bit of damage to the crystal itself now, as though it was dropped at some stage, or perhaps an animal struck it while walking

through the water, but the crack is just to one side and takes nothing away from its strange beauty. Lord Waterford did not recall when or how it was damaged. It was probably long before his time.

He did remember it being used when the cattle were in danger from disease such as foot and mouth. 'There is no longer any call for it to be used now', he said, 'as modern medicine has caught up with the healing and prevention of disease in the animals'. So it rests quietly, unused, but still held in special respect as a wonder from past times.

When I asked if it was permitted for me to hold the crystal Lord Waterford had no objection at all. So with great excitement I lifted this strange healing crystal into my hands. I have often handled crystals, used for healing, and am sensitive to their energy but this time there was a strange inertness to the crystal. There was a flat, blanking sensation, a small spark of white light, for a split second, then nothing. Perhaps the crack has interfered with its energy or more realistically it was not for human healing energies but for animal energies.

There is another old belief about the binding of energy with silver; so many things we do not understand.

I placed the crystal back on the timber chest and showed his lordship the book which referred to it. He was very interested in what it said and I left him a copy of the piece.

I am very appreciative of his kindness in allowing me to see and touch the ancient piece of crystal.

*\* Godfrey de Bouillon took part in one of the first crusades. He fought many serious battles but his main aim was to aid in the restoration of the Holy Land to Christian rule. His army took back the city of Jerusalem in July 1099. He died in the year 1100.*

## THE SHELL HOUSE IN CURRAGHMORE

There are many stories associated with Curraghmore Estate. The Shell House, which is situated in the beautiful gardens, near to the main house, is almost concealed by shrubbery. It is a surprise, waiting to enchant you, with its fairy-tale appearance.

It is old, but still beautiful, and carefully maintained. It was built in 1754, as a Folly, by Catherine, Countess of Tyrone. She was totally involved in the decoration, and her 'hands-on' project is said to have taken her 261 days to complete. It was a huge undertaking for any one person but her enthusiasm and artistic talent created a fabulous work of art which has withstood the passage of time.

The story goes that Lady Catherine, herself, charged the captains of ships, leaving the Port of Waterford, to collect and return shells to her from all over the world. Many kindly captains indulged the request from the lovely, Lady Catherine, and scientific examination of the shells in recent times tell us that many of the exotic and rare varieties of shells used in the decoration of the Shell House, do indeed, come from all around the world.

The sailing ships of the time would have been engaged in the Seven Years War and would have carried canon for protection. Armed in similar fashion were the merchant ships, which carried goods to every corner of the world, including the Orient. It was a dangerous time to be at sea and full credit is due, to the men who took time to remember the request of Lady Catherine. But the good lady had made a lasting impression on the captains and it is also likely, that they would have visited and dined at Curraghmore House.

It is said that she was very beautiful and her husband commissioned a statue of the countess to be sculpted by the famous artist John van Nost. This statue can be seen today within the Shell House.

At the time when Lady Catherine was engaged in decorating the Shell House the surrounding countryside would have seen political unrest, of an agrarian nature. A society, known as Whiteboys, was active in Waterford and the surrounding counties. They were seeking fair rents and fair laws, with regard to leasing and owning land. This involved violent encounters between Whiteboys and the law.

## THE OLD CARRIGANURE FOX

A notable character in the hunting lore of the area was the old fox of Carriganure, who fell on 29 October 1907, the second day of the hunting season, having given the Waterford Hounds a series of extraordinary runs during the previous two seasons.

Among them was a hunting run of three hours and five minutes on 18 January 1906 covering 20 miles of country. On 19 February 1907 Lord Waterford had to stop the hounds in the dark after a pursuit of three hours and twenty minutes, again over 20 miles of country. They drew him again on 26 February 1907, when he achieved his crowning glory by defeating hounds after four hours thirty-eight minutes. The hounds must have covered 30 miles and some horsemen said they covered 40 miles that day.

His last effort was not bad; after one hour and four minutes he was pulled down fairly, in open ground near Ballyriteen, according to Mr Will Hynes.

On 8 March 1906 by crossing and re-crossing the railway the fox had deflected the hounds into the rocks in Darrigal Woods. Lord Waterford had high netting placed around this place, to make sure of him for the next run. However, the fox ran for the big sheet of water at Pouldrew and swam across it and got into Mount Congreve.

The fox was unmistakable in appearance, except for the covert keeper no one knew him better than Mr Arthur Hunt of Rocklands.

The following verses record the great hunt of the Carriganure Fox:

Come all ye sporting gentlemen and listen to my song
It's only a few verses and I won't delay you long,
Concerning this awful run of forty miles or more
With the greyhound fox from Carriganure
And the hounds from Curraghmore

On the day they held this famous run
There was a splendid meet
But these gentlemen have horses to keep Reynard on his feet
Carriganure is then first drawn
This famous fox lied there
He can scour the hills and valleys far better than a hare.

The fox he broke in Hackettstown and the first man that I saw
Was Mr George F. Malcolmson, a native of Portlaw.
They first made for Rathanny and then for Lissahaney
And if the wind will favour him he will go on for Bunmahon.

A man named Robert Phelan feeds this fox with care
And keeps him in his lurking place until the hounds come there
For there he lies in ambush until anything comes across
But he has to rise and shake his brush, when they meet in Carroll's Cross

I must congratulate these horsemen with the dogs, and the Master
of them too
For they are as fast as any greyhound that ran in Waterloo
Power and Capt. Getting are as good as you can find
For when the Tally Ho is on they are never far behind.

And now my song is ended and I leave my pen aside
For the men who hunt this famous fox there is no mistake, can ride.
And they will do next season as they have done before
Likewise the noble Marquis the pride of Curraghmore.

*Taken from parish book* – Ballyduff-Kilmeaden Portrait of a Parish
*by Michael Carberry, edited by Donnchadh O Ceallachain (in asso-*
*ciation with Des Cowman), published by Ballyduff Parish Council,*
*Ballyduff Lower, Kilmeaden, Co. Waterford, © 1998. Reprinted here*
*by kind permission of Ballyduff Parish Council.*

# Ten

# FAMOUS
# OUTLAWS

### CROTTY THE HIGHWAYMAN

When I was young we used to swap comics. I don't think anyone does that any more. But we had no television then – and for a long while we had no electricity either, so reading comics was mostly done in daylight because at night you would only have an oil lamp or candles or sometimes a good fire would brighten up the kitchen.

Well one of the comics doing the rounds then was about the highwayman, Dick Turpin. We were all on his side, by the way. So it was no wonder that once we finished saying the rosary and everything was tidied up, we would talk about highwaymen. We even knew where there was a big oak branch stretching out across the road, near my grandfather's place, that perhaps a highwayman could hide and jump down on a passing horse-drawn coach. It was then that my Dad, or my brother, both in Heaven now, bless them, would start to talk about a real highwayman and we would listen, with our ears out on stalks and our eyes as wide as saucers.

The story was true in all the basic facts. William Crotty was a highwayman, who lived and loved and robbed the rich, in and around the Comeragh Mountains, in Co. Waterford. But sure that was not the real story we wanted to hear. We needed details and so they were supplied, with enthusiasm, embroidered and exciting.

William Crotty was once young and playful as any child. But he lived in a time when the Redcoats were the hand of the English in Ireland. That was in the 1700s, a terrible long time ago. The Redcoats were never very good to the ordinary people and life was hard. There were no factories or places of work out there then and the people struggled to make a living from the land and the skills of their hands and minds. Work with landowners and farmers was difficult to get and poverty was ever at their doors.

Some of the lads who grew up with William Crotty went off to sea, some to fish and others to join the British Navy and climb the riggings of tall ships used in battle. More became sailors who sailed the world on merchant ships. It was a life that never appealed to William. He loved his own place and particularly he loved the Comeragh Mountains. He knew them like the back of his hand as he had roamed them high and low since he was a lad.

It used to torment him sorely to see the horse-drawn carriages pass by with their fancy lords and ladies in their grand clothes. Sure wouldn't anyone feel the same? It was a time when there was a huge divide in society. The 'haves' (who would never part with a penny, if they could help it and thought poor people were less than animals) and the 'have nots' (who, God help them, didn't even have a penny). Cruel hard times make for cruel hard decisions and that was how William Crotty made his choice. He would stay in his own area and he would do his living best to try and help his own people.

Everyone, who could, had a horse or a donkey and William had for himself a fairly decent horse. They took care of their animals then as they depended on them for so many things. It was easier then to get weapons and so he armed himself and his few followers and they began to wage war on the aristocrats who journeyed through the area and even further afield where rich merchants came and went to Waterford City itself.

The first robbery they carried out must have been terrifying for everyone. Their hearts would have been thumping like drums with fear and excitement. They were doing it for real this time, not just talking about it. The fear in their victims faces probably amazed them first and then gave them a great sense of power over their hated enemies. Riding away from that first raid must have been exhilarating and heart-stopping at the same time. It was always his way to share out whatever he managed to steal back from the rich and this too, must have often, caused problems with his followers.

As I said earlier, he was young and in the whole of his health and so it is no wonder that he got married. He had probably known his wife since they were children because she too, lived in the area of the Comeraghs. In the early days, it was still safe for him and his followers to disperse to their own homes when a raid was over, but as time went by and it became more and more dangerous for them. Crotty had to make some other arrangements.

He found himself a hideout up high in the mountains. It was a cave where the only access was by rope from high above. Below that there

was the cold water of the lake which became known as Crotty's lake. On the top of the cliffs, high above he could, on a clear day, see for many miles in every direction, which was a great help to him. On a foggy day it was just dangerous and no one could get to him anyway.

One of his strategies when he was being hunted was to turn the shoes on his horse the opposite way round and so when he was flying away from them his horse's shoe marks showed him going in the opposite direction. It confounded the Redcoats many times. But they knew the general area he came from and were giving the poor people in the area around the Comeraghs a terrible time, coming in upon their little cottages, with their muskets and bayonets and causing all sort of upset and harm.

The locals had great time for Crotty and his men at first but then life became very difficult for them and they were under constant pressure. It was said that he frequented a local tavern at Dá Reu's Cross and didn't seem to notice that people were getting more afraid when he was around.

Well, the Redcoats had failed to catch Crotty for a good number of years and now they tried a different tack. They began to put pressure on individuals, and they convinced one of Crotty's old friends, a man by the name of David Norris, that it would be better for him and his if he betrayed Crotty. It was a time of great savagery when things, such as the rack, the pitch cap, boiling oil, and other forms of torture and maiming were employed by those in power so we can just imagine what happened.

However it was, David Norris met with Crotty at his hideout, the cave, up in the mountains. They talked and drank together. Crotty drinking more than was good for him fell asleep and while he was out to the world David Norris wet his gunpowder and took away his knife. He then signalled to the waiting Redcoats and they came and took Crotty. It was the cold bitter month of February and the date was the 16th in the year of our Lord 1742.

Did Norris meet his friend's eyes as he was hauled away down the mountainside? I often wondered. Did he collect the bounty which was on Crotty's head or did he lose himself among the sailors who left the local ports?

It was a month before Crotty appeared before the Assizes in Waterford. Lying in that miserable gaol he must have hoped and hoped for escape or rescue but it never happened. He was dragged up before the judge and sentenced in short order to be hanged and quartered and his head cut off and to be fixed to one of the spikes over the gate of the County Gaol, as a warning to other thieves and highwaymen. It was a brutal time.

There ended the life of William Crotty, the young boy who loved the Comeragh Mountains. It is said that he always stashed away some of his takings in a secret place in the mountains. If it has ever been found we do not know, but it is possible that it may still be there or indeed long gone.

His gruesome death left behind a widow and child who were, in turn, hunted by the Redcoats. It is said that so terrifying did this become that she threw herself and her child off the top of the cliff, known as Crotty's Rock, killing them both, rather than face the torture and death at the hands of the Redcoats.

There is also a lament for William Crotty, which was said to have been written by his wife while he was in gaol. But Lord knows where she would have found time to do this, if she was on the run from his enemies. The words were put to an old Gaeilge air.

William Crotty I often told you
That David Norris would come 'round you.
In your bed where you lay sleeping,
And leave me here in sorrow weeping.
Ochone, ochone, ochone, oh.
He wet your powder, he stole your arms,
And left you helpless in the midst of alarms.
My bitter curse on him and his,
That brought you to and end like this.
Ochone, ochone, ochone, oh.
Oh the judge but he was cruel,
Refusing a long day to my jewel.
Sure I thought that would be, maybe
See the face of your poor baby.

But tempter's gold and traitors, greedy,
Have left the poor and lowly needy.
'Twas you that heard the widow sighing,
'Twas you that heard the orphan crying.
Strong brave and true and kind to women,
Yet fierce and dread to Saxon foeman.
As thou tonight in gaol you're sleeping,
And oh I'm left in sorrow weeping
Ochone, ochone, ochone, oh.
O'er Coumshingaun the dark clouds gather,
You'll sleep no more among the heather.
Through the Comeraghs hills the night winds are sighing,
Where oft you sent the Redcoats flying
Ochone, ochone, ochone, oh.
Ahearn's gold bought Norris over,
That night the Redcoats round your cover.
May heaven's vengeance o'er them gather,
My baby ne'er shall see its father
Ochone, ochone, ochone, oh.

*A ballad called 'The Tears in Mary's Eyes' was composed, in 2009, by Billy McBolan and this looks at Crotty's last minutes before he is hanged.*

## THE CONNERYS

I was over near Cappoquin to visit Mount Mellary when I fell into talk with a local woman, who was curious about what I was jotting down in my notebook. When I told her I was following old stories from Co. Waterford she laughed and said she hoped I would not forget the musical Connerys. She knew by my face that I had no idea who the musical Connerys were and proceeded to give me the following tale. I took it with a grain of salt and I hope you will too.

The Connery brothers were named James, John and Patrick and there was a girl in the family too. The girl seems to have lived fairly circumspectly for she is not mentioned any more in the story. The brothers, on the other hand, were very lively in their pursuits and were fond of Faction Fighting. It was all the go in Munster and indeed, in other parts of the country. 'Ireland was awash with young men rearing to go,' said she.

She looked like a woman who might know a thing or two so I kept listening. With great relish, she proceeded to tell me all about how the different factions named themselves. The most famous were The Seanvest and The Caravat and they wore different regalia to identify themselves to each other. 'Young fellows, they would make you laugh, wouldn't they?' says she, with her eye on my pen moving on the notebook.

Then there were The Gows and The Poleens. The Connery boys were with the Poleens and often came home with cuts and welts raised on them from sceilps received during the fighting. It was great sport as long as you didn't get killed.

'But sure,' says she, 'isn't there always someone to spoil everything. All the grand lads fighting and this fellow goes off and gets himself killed, stone dead, at the fair in Ballykeroge.' She waved her hand in the direction of Dungarvan and I understood that Ballykeroge was somewhere between Cappoquin and Dungarvan. That was when the trouble began for the Connery boys. The man who died was from The Gows and this divided people much more than before. The Connery boys were accused of murder but they were acquitted.

'Ah but they were grand singers and musicians,' she told me. 'They could make every man in the pub stop talking when they played or raised their voices in song.' They seem to have frequented many pubs in their day, for the next man killed was a David Tobin, when a row arose in a bar. The dead man's wife gave evidence against John Connery. Once again the judge ruled in favour of Connery and he was found not guilty. But they were getting a very bad reputation now, despite the music and the grand lads they were.

They had enemies and the Faction Fighting was no longer the 'sport' where a cracked skull would not kill you. There were many out there who didn't like the way things always fell out in favour of the Connerys, and one, more dangerous than the rest, was a legal man. 'He knew his books, he did,' she declared. 'He was out to get the Connerys, one way or another, so when James was arrested and brought before the Waterford Assizes, for the attempted murder of a man called Hackett, things changed. Hackett worked for this solicitor called Thomas Foley, who was from Lismore. Hackett swore he recognised James Connery, even though his attackers wore women's clothing and had blackened faces. 'Sure,' said she, 'he didn't know a Connery from a bar of soap.' She shook her head disgustedly. 'Hackett was only doing what his boss, Foley, told him. There was another witness, a grand man,' says she, 'and he gave the judge and jury so many different sides to the story that he ended up getting himself sentenced to seven years' transportation, for perjury. Ah, well, that's how it goes sometimes.' She sighed as though it was yesterday, and she knew them all well, and not over 180 years previously, in the year 1835.

'James Connery, the eldest lad, him with the lovely eyes,' says she 'was sentenced to be transported for the rest of his life to Botany Bay. The Devil mend the lot of them'.

Well, after that it was a story of narrow escapes and getting caught and escaping again and again. It was her belief that the Governor of Waterford Jail was in sympathy with the Connerys and The Poleens, for didn't they escape, with a gang of other prisoners, from Waterford Jail when he was in charge. Then again, another time when the same Governor, a man called Bruce, was taking them to Queenstown for transportation, didn't they escape when they manage to climb a high wall in Clogheen Police Station. She was grim when she pronounced that it was Foley, from Lismore, who made sure that Governor Bruce lost his grand job and he not a bad man at all.

There was another time when they were almost caught drinking in a country pub and singing, when, not far from where we were standing at that blessed minute, they managed to swim the river Blackwater and escape. 'They were great swimmers, grand figures of men.' By this time I understood that she was very fond of young strong men.

'Sometimes', she said, 'the grand boys of the Connerys had to be stern with informers and they would write, or get someone else to write, a note and send it to the informer saying that they would be coming for them soon and things like that.'

'One time', she said, 'they decided that they would like to get back to normal life and they approached the Co. Waterford Lt Hon. Henry Villiers Stuart. They asked him to put in a word for them and see if he could get them a pardon, if they agreed to leave the country. Villiers Stuart was no soft touch, he sent for the police at once. The grand young men had to run for their lives, away through the woods.'

Her face was sombre when she finished her story. 'It was their own daftness that caught them in the end. They were in the pub doing what they liked best, singing and drinking, when the local police came in searching for a sheep-stealing blackguard. They recognised the Connery lads and arrested them on the spot. There was no escape this time. They were sentenced to transportation and so it happened in 1837.'

'They were young,' she said sadly, 'John was only thirty years of age and Patrick was forty years. There was a song about them', she remembered, and began to hum a tune I vaguely recognised but she could not remember the words except some in Gaeilge.

I asked her name and she smiled 'Some call me Mary the Memory, for I remember more than is good for me. I love the old yarns, about the gallant young men.'

*It is possible to access more historically accurate stories about the Connery brothers on the internet, and there are many versions of songs which refer to them also.*

# Eleven

# ROCKETT'S CASTLE

*There is a time of the year when the little fishing cots, on the River Suir, put out and cast their nets. The days for this are getting shorter and shorter. But during the 1970s and '80s there were many days when I was on the river with them. A grand fraternity of fishermen putting out from Polerone and, barring snags, they would catch a salmon or two, or the younger fish, called peel. It was on the river I first caught sight of Rockett's Castle. It was an old ruin on the banks of the river in an area now known as Mayfield.*

*Having an interest in all these ancient things, I asked the fishermen what they knew about the ruined edifice. Between them they gave me their versions of the story attached to it, and my conclusion is that just when you think you know a lot you find you know nothing at all.*

Rockett's Castle was built during the Norman Invasion. They were great builders, those same Normans, and many of their strong places are still standing. When Dermot MacMurrough invited them over to help him, little did he know what he was starting.

Well the man who was set up in this particular little castle was called de la Rochelle or, as he was called locally, Rockett. The Irish were never into the fancy French titles. This was all during the time of the Crusades so it was a very long time ago. Some people have put the date of Rockett's Castle at around the early 1200s. You would think that a small little castle, far up along the River Suir, would be a safe enough place for anyone, but in those times the rivers were the highways on which most people travelled, especially invading forces. Religion was also a cause of contention between peoples and nations, God help us.

Now to get on with the story, the man called de la Rochelle was by all accounts a fair and good man but he was not a favourite of his neighbour, the Earl of Ormond, who was the most powerful man on the other side of the river and all the way up to Kilkenny. The grand little castle caught the eye of the Earl and with the blessing of King Charles I of England, he made war on Rockett and after a bitter struggle took possession of the castle and scattered its inhabitants. Rockett was now on the run and being a man of his time he took to the sea to escape from the persecutions of the Earl of Ormond.

The ships then were all sailing vessels and they were used to carry everything of value from one place to another. They were also used as warships and were armed with cannon. So the enterprising Rockett decided that the only way he could fight back against those who had put him out of his castle was to turn pirate. Being a pirate then was common enough as times were very hard on most people and who could blame him, for he must have been fair scalded at the way he was treated. He also had great pity for the people, especially the Catholics, who were suffering badly under the new rule. It is said that he was generous with the wealth he captured and local people benefited often from his pirating forays.

His pirating activities were aimed solely at the English ships. Wasn't he a grand man. He knew a bad enemy when he saw one. He harried them up and down the coast of Ireland and became a terrible thorn in their sides. Maybe he would have been better off pirating off the French coast or even clearing off to the Indian Ocean. But no, he stuck near to home, in his hatred of the English. It was his undoing, for a large bounty was placed on his head and that of his crew. Desperate people make desperate enemies and a reward was a temptation to someone, so eventually Rockett and his crew were caught and brought up before the English justice.

All this sounds like it might have happened in an old story book but it was real enough and there are records kept of old court cases held here in Waterford. The English were great for keeping records of their mighty conquests and poor Rockett came under their notice. There was a terrible savagery to law and order under the invaders. Rockett was, by all accounts hanged, drawn and quartered and then beheaded. Bless us and save us, did they think he would rise again?

His head was placed on a spike at the city gates of Waterford and according to legend there was a notice placed on it saying 'Beware do not offend your king'. Charles I must have been a terrible man indeed.

There is another part to this legend which bears a mention. It would have been outside the walls of the city that the executions of the time would have taken place, and there is a story about one area, known as 'Crann a Riocoidig' which literally means Rockett's Tree, where it is said the gruesome execution was completed. A man called Christy Brophy from the Yellow Road Band (Thomas Meagher Fife & Drum Band) told me that the Yellow Road was the area where Rockett was executed, and that it was given its name from all the yellow gorse blossoms which grew along the wayside.

Rockett's Castle passed down through many generations and when a man known as Sir Algernon May owned it he called the area around it Mayfield and that name still holds there to this day. At that time it was described as a 'fortress manor house'. It was a building with five floors and thick walls surrounding it. Why it was such a source of annoyance to many generations is a wonder, for eventually it was destroyed, sometime during the late seventeenth century.

But lands and ruins are always desirable and in more recent times the manor house and castle have been renovated once more by a different type of invader. We now have the wealthy foreign buyers coming into Ireland, and, to give them their due, they have done a lot of work on Rockett's Castle. It is now a shooting and fishing estate. A fine lake to the front of the house has been stocked with fish and there is a sense of renewal and all sorts of possibilities yet for the little castle. May future generations be kind to it.

Twelve

# THE STORY OF
# DUNHILL CASTLE

You never want to meet a Dunhill man on the hurling pitch. They are fierce persevering men and it seems it was always so. Even the stones of the castle they once built still stubbornly refuse to give way.

The name Dunhill, they tell me, comes from the old name Dún Aill, which most probably meant it was a fort owned by a chieftain called Aill, or on the other hand it just meant Fort of the Rock. Whatever its original name it was changed to Dunhill as time went by.

Our ancestors loved to build in high places, be they saints, scholars or just important or frightened men. A fort or a dún could sit on hill in comfort and those within could relax, to some extent, for they would have ample warning of an attack of any kind.

Forts, by their very nature, drew to themselves people looking for protection. Those who did not live within its protective structure, for one reason or another, would set up home within a safe distance so they could get inside if the danger was real. The animals, grain, firewood and fodder would all be hurried in out of harm's way. So a settlement grew up around Dunhill in the early days.

With the passage of centuries this very handy, high place became the ideal site for a castle and it was built on the orders of the la Poer family, who were the strong landowners in the Dunhill area in the early 1200s.

It was raised by the men of the area and was a great undertaking. Many a good man sweated long and hard in its building and as my mother, God be good to her, would say, 'Not one of them has a pain in his head this day'.

It perched high above a little winding road and overlooked the River Anne, which enters the sea at Annestown, a good way further on. In it's heyday you could see anyone approaching, no matter from what direction they came. It was built when castles were needed and indeed in fashion, if such a thing can be said about castles. Anyone who owned a lot of land found it very handy to have a castle to retire to when someone tried to take the land away from them. But the self-same castles acted like red rags to bulls, in some cases, and again and again people tried to take them for themselves.

Dunhill Castle was very grand when it was finished, with all the necessary protection set in place and its builders saw the la Poers take up residence.

It was a good thing that those who lived in the area were of hardy stock for the new dwellers were of a fierce and warlike disposition. They were of Norman stock, the la Poers, but sure you knew that anyway. In the fourteenth century, it is recorded, they made many forays out from Dunhill. They thought nothing of attacking the City of Waterford, not once or twice, but as often as the notion took them or their descendants.

However, by the year 1345 the good citizens of that city were better able to defend themselves and after a devastating raid, in and around Waterford, a counter attack was launched against them and the la Poers, who were caught on that raid, were taken and hanged. Waterford was always a great place for hanging and other gruesome ways of disposing of enemies, both real and perceived.

Not all the la Poers were caught and those who still held the castle joined forces with the O'Driscoll family, another clan not to be trifled with. Strengthened by the alliance, the old way of life continued: raid, retreat, and raid again. Sometimes the Dunhill men succeeded and sometimes they retreated gratefully within the strong walls of their castle, to bide their time for a while. It was after a battle in Tramore in the year 1368 that the powers of Kilmeaden took ownership of Dunhill Castle. They were all related, you see.

The castle was managed well up until the arrival of Cromwell. By all rights he shouldn't even have noticed it and he on his way between Waterford and Cork but notice it he did. He paid it a lot of attention. Any castle along the way was a legitimate target for his marauding force.

Now it just happened that it was the wife of Lord John Power who was in residence in Dunhill when Cromwell attacked and laid siege to the castle. Her husband was protecting their castle in Kilmeaden. Gyles was the name she went by and she managed to defend the castle for quite a time, and the story goes that Cromwell was on the point of giving up when the woman lost the run of herself entirely.

The one thing you don't do in the middle of a siege is fall out with your own military. She is said to have given orders that the men on the walls were not to get wine, which was the drink of the time, but were to be given buttermilk instead. Maybe she was afraid they would fall asleep with the drink or maybe she just didn't have any wine left. But, if we are to believe the tale, when the gunnery engineer received this order, he took it very badly. Indeed he took it so sorely that he raised the white flag, opened the gates and surrendered the castle. Ah, isn't drink a terrible curse? Sure he probably wasn't even a local.

Cromwell was delighted, don't you know, when he saw the way things were unfolding, and why wouldn't he be? He probably couldn't believe his luck. But he was curious and the first thing he wanted to know was why they had surrendered. When the bold bucko who ran up the white flag explained about the drink Cromwell was not impressed. He had no time for winos and less entirely for traitors, be they on his side or the other, so he had him executed on the spot. Not many survived the taking of Dunhill Castle by Cromwell in 1649.

The castle and lands were given over eventually to a Sir John Cole. Neither he nor his family ever lived in the castle and could you blame them. It must have been in a terrible state after the siege

and the slaughter afterwards. Whatever the reason, in the years that followed, it slowly began to succumb to the lack of·care and the ravages of the weather. By the early 1800s it was in ruins. All that sweat, blood and tears brought to nothing by Mother Nature in the end.

If ghosts walk there, surely one is of the 'buttermilk gunner' and another the Countess Gyles. Peace reigns now over Dunhill and only the ivy-clad walls, which remain standing, give any hint of a more troubled time in the past.

When you think of it, here we are now and some of the ancient walls and tower are still standing. The men of Dunhill, bless them, were great builders.

# Thirteen

# AN
# BÍDEACH

*This story is an interpretation of a story by the first President of Ireland, Dr Douglas Hyde. I got this version from Master Storyteller, Liam Murphy of Waterford, who had adapted it to suit his own place. I hope I can do it justice.*

The *Bídeach* lived with his mother on the peninsula of Rinn an gCunach, across the bay from the town of Dungarvan. From birth he had never grown any more than eighteen inches and his mother had reared him in cotton wool, tended to his every need and reared him without the benefit of school. She was probably afraid, the *cratur*, in case anyone might step on him.

The *Bídeach* never went far from the house but, even in his thirty-ninth year, he was happy as a sunbeam. He had never been to church, chapel or meeting, or to the town of Dungarvan. His mother warned him to 'beware of the women of that place, the way they might look at you and, heaven forbid, that they might wink at you'. His mother repeated her warning, 'Beware of the women of Dungarvan, if they wink at you.'

One day, shortly after his thirty-ninth birthday, his mother had to go into Dungarvan to make arrangements. She prepared porridge, meat sandwiches, lemonade and sweet tea and as she set off in the ass and cart she again warned the *Bideach* to stay and to speak to no one, no matter who called. He promised and promised, and why wouldn't he, and he living in the lap of luxury. When the mother was out of sight he settled down in comfort and stretched out in the sunbeams dancing through the windows, such was his delight, until a dark shadow crossed the sky and fear leapt to his heart as down the grassy boreen to the cottage came a tall dark man of bad temper, astride an *asal beag dubh*, a little black ass. He beat the ass and urged it forward

'Don't buckle under me now', he cried as they turned into the yard and he cried out 'Come out this instant, *Bideach*. Come out now.'

How did he know the *Bideach*'s name? I tell you this, some people know a lot more than they let on, and the tall dark man of the Formoire knew more than his prayers.

'Come out *Bideach* or it will be the worse for you.'

The *Bideach* shook with fear and went to hide behind the pot in the hearth.

The tall dark man kicked in the door and strode in across the flags of the floor.

'Where are you my little *Bideach*? Come out now like a good little man or it will be the worse for you. Come out.'

The *Bideach*'s little heart was crossways in him, from fear; there was no escape. He looked this way and that, and the only daylight he could see was between the tall dark man's legs. Without waiting to think, he made a dash for the door, straight out between those gigantic legs. The man was not expecting this, and as he tried to grab at the flying figure of the panic-stricken *Bideach*, scooting out between his legs, didn't he trip himself up and came crashing down. Sprawled across the flagstone floor he fell, splitting his head on the hearthstone.

The *Bideach* had won clear, and shot out the door into the sunlight beyond, panting and gasping until he thought his heart would pop out through his little jacket. He stopped at the far wall of the garden and realised that he was not followed. Hands on his little knees he rested for a few minutes and there was still no sign of the man.

Though still in fear, curiosity got the better of him and he gathered his courage again and crept back up to the broken door. Oh, mile a murder, what did he see? Only the long fellow stretched across the floor and his head in smithereens against the hearthstone. His first thought was for his Mammy. She will kill me, look at the state of the place, and she after telling me not to let anyone in. What will I do, what will I do at all? The door is broken and a dead man in around her kitchen.

Now, in all this world, the only thing the *Bideach* feared was that his Mammy would be upset. So gathering strength from somewhere deep inside his little chest, he grabbed the long fellow by the two legs and pulled and pulled until he managed to drag him out over the broken door and around the side of the little house, where his Mammy wouldn't see him when she came back from Dungarvan. He might mend the door, in time, when a voice spoke beside him.

The poor little *cratur* nearly leapt out of his skin, the fright he got.

'Well done *Bideach*, well done. You did a good deed this day to rid me of that torment from off my back.'

Try as he might, in his fear, the *Bideach* could see no one but the *asal beag dubh*, who was indeed speaking to him.

'Don't be afraid', said the ass. 'Don't be afraid for I am a Prince of old Ireland, trapped by a curse in the body of this ass, by the tall dark man of the Formoire, and if you can do just one more favour for me, I can be set free and go back to helping my father, the king. If you do this one thing for me now I will reward you beyond measure or pleasure.'

Still in a dazed state, the Bideach found himself up on the back of the *asal beag dubh*, going like the March wind across the country, until they arrived at the Penitential Island of Lough Derg.

'I will be released from my curse if you can go around this island, from shrine to shrine, on your knees, and pray for me and the poor souls who need our prayers. Do this deed tonight and in the morning I will be restored and your reward will be waiting for you at home.'

As trusting as ever the *Bideach* did as he was bid, and, even though his knees were cut and blistered, he completed his task.

He was greeted by a warrior Prince who said, 'Close your eyes and you will be back home, back home in your yard at Rinn an gCunach. Down your boreen will come the Herd of Plenty led by a golden sow. Climb up on that sow's back and put your hand into her right ear and a silk purse will be your reward, a silk purse from a sow's ear, which will never empty, no matter how much gold you take from it.'

In the shudder of the wind the *Bideach* found himself back in his mother's house. There was no sign of the tall dark man and the door stood as good as new, with no sign of any damage. The *Bideach* let out a long breath and just then, down the *boreen* came the Herd of Plenty. They were thundering towards him and he knew that the only chance he had of getting up on the golden sow's back was to make a run for the little wall by the gate. He made it just in time and took a flying leap and landed safely. Sure, to a little man, like himself, the pig's back was a great place to be. He climbed up until he could put his little hand into her ear and sure enough he drew out the silk purse of plenty, just as he had been told.

Such was his delight that when his Mammy came home, shortly afterwards, he told her the whole story. Well wasn't she delighted herself, bless her, and why wouldn't she? And such is the way with money and them that have it, the name of the *Bideach* spread far and wide. His generosity was legendary, and people travelled the length and breadth of Ireland to call at the *Bideach*'s house, and they never went away wanting.

It is said that St Patrick called when he was building the cathedral in Ard Macha, and went away with a *flúirse* of gold.

Now we come to the sad part of the story, and isn't there often a sad turning in our own story too? The *Bideach*'s mother died and was buried with a High Mass of Bishops and clerics, and in his sadness and loss the *Bideach* resolved to go to the town of Dungarvan, as he had never been there when his mother was alive. Sure, he forgot the dear woman's warning and he delighted in the women of Dungarvan, who did wink at him, and tickled him under the chin as well. He soon cheered up and fell head over heels in love with a girl with summer eyes, golden laughter and a wink that would charm even the hardest heart. Before the harvest was ripe they were inseparable, and under a warm harvest moon they married and settled down in Rinn an gCunach.

The *Bideach* was never happier and he lavished fistfuls of gold on his new wife and his purse never grew less. They spent days whispering in each other's ears, and at night she would nibble the *Bideach*'s ear and tell him how wonderful he was.

In the first chill of winter she stopped her nibbling and whispering and began to make demands. 'If you loved me you would let me take the purse with me to the town of Dungarvan, where my friends could see how much you love me and trust me.'

Sometimes she would snap at his head, and bit by bit the *Bideach* relented and in the end he gave his wife the purse, to shop on her own. She hugged him in delight and rushed to show off in the Square in Dungarvan, buying bolts of material and expensive folderols and filligree gee gaws and fripperies of every colour. When the time came to pay for her treasures she took out the purse, the silk purse of plenty, and plunged her hand deep into it and took out only a handful of stones. She recoiled in shock and howled in rage, as time and again, only gravel fell from her fingers. She rushed to the *Bideach* and attacked him.

'You have shamed me before the world and the town of Dungarvan. Made me a laughing stock and a mockery. Put it right at once!'

The poor *Bideach*, who was indeed poor now, put hand into the purse and got only stones. The magic, like love, was gone out the window. A chill struck his heart as his wife turned on her heels and walked out of his life forever.

'I should never have married you, you little maneen, you little *Bideach* you. Me mother was right; small men are useless.' With a chill in his heart the *Bideach* took to his bed. His sadness and loss broke his little heart. With his last remaining breath he took the purse and hurled it up into the stormy south-west wind, which carried it away in towards Waterford.

Where it landed no one saw, but the story goes that a Tree of Plenty grew up on that spot. Many have searched for it, to no avail. To this very day some people who hear this story believe that their lives could be changed, if only they could find it, as if a story could change anybody's life anyhow.

# 14

# SLABHRA NA FÍRINNE – THE CHAIN OF TRUTH

*This story could have originated in any country in the world. It is told in Arab countries in a slightly different form but I am sure it must have begun in Ireland, when God was a boy, for haven't we still got the hill to prove it. If you doubt me, let you follow the River Suir as far as Carrick-on-Suir and there you will see it for yourself, and it called* Sliabh na mBan.

Long, long ago, at the dawn of time, when God was a boy, only learning his trade, and Éire young, there was a place in Ireland which was a wonder to the world. The Hill of Truth. It was in this place the young God let down from heaven a chain of gold and if you told a lie while holding on to this chain you would be burnt to ashes. God bless us and save us all.

Well, there was a man and a beautiful woman, married happily, in Portlaw, which is in Co. Waterford. It rests snugly in beneath the thickly wooded hills of Curraghmore Estate, with the little River Clodagh hurrying, through the village, to meet the River Suir just beyond it. Joseph and Aisling were their names.

Every morning Joseph went off to work, making tables and chairs and other nice pieces of furniture, in the little workshop he had out the Carrick road. After saying goodbye to her man, the beautiful Aisling would clean and scrub her little home. She would

make sure she had the fire cleaned out and the ashes away outside before lunchtime, not to bring the bad luck. She would scrub the front step and anything that would wait for her before making grand dinners for them, for she loved to cook. Some men have all the luck. Sometimes she would take a break and go walking through the woods, picking flowers and broscain for the fire. Life continued like this for a couple of years but they were never blessed with children and Aisling became dissatisfied. Lord help us all.

It was hard on her, the *cratur*, going down for the water at the village well and meeting with all the other young women she had gone to school with, and they with babies on their hips or by the hand and maybe carrying again, bless us and save us. At first it wasn't something that anyone passed a remark on, but there is always one spiteful hussy in every community, and so it began as little digs like 'Have you any news yet Aisling?', then eventually reached the stage where if she admired a child, they would say, 'Sure what do you know of children.' It nearly broke her heart but she never let on to her husband that she minded at all. She just avoided people and got the water early or late after they were gone.

After a while this beautiful, lonely woman met another man, while she was going through the wood. Sean was his name and soon they were meeting in the wood regularly. They liked to talk and little by little they began to fall in love. That's how life is sometimes. Well Sean began to call to the happy little house, when the husband was out working, so that he could spend some time with the beautiful Aisling. Life became very pleasant for a time, for everyone. The beautiful woman would spend the morning working in the house, cleaning and scrubbing doing all the little things which made life good. In the afternoon her man friend would call and they would spend time together and by the time her husband came home, she would have the dinner ready and be contentedly waiting for him and the glow of love about her.

Little by little the whispers started. There are people in every corner of the world and they have nothing else to do only whisper about everyone else's business and that is what happened here. One of the local 'old biddies' started it. She looked at Aisling as she passed and remarked loudly, that no married woman should look that contented. There had to be something wrong there, and so it progressed. Everyone began to notice just how joyful Aisling looked, and there was no sign that she was with child either. No, they decided she had no right to look so pleased with herself, no right at all. So it is nothing new that when people settle down on their pillows that they would recount their day's happenings, so word spread like wildfire. Aisling was up to something but no one could prove it.

When Joseph went to the local Seanti, to have a drink, in the evening, there would be whispers behind hands, sudden laughs and eventually someone, too far gone in their cups to be circumspect, said it outright that he had heard that the beautiful Aisling had a new man friend. Well, the blood drained from Joseph's face as he turned to face him. The man realised he had crossed a boundary and murmured that they just knew there was another man in her life. There had to be, after all, she was too contented according to the older women, and old women knew these things. He backed away and was gone out the door before Joseph could say a word. Well, once it was out in public, Joseph felt obliged to confront his lovely wife even though he himself would never doubt her, but still.

So he went home and, because of the kind of people they were, he asked her straight out if there was any truth in the rumours he had heard. Need I tell you she got a bit of a start but straight away pulled herself together and began to cry. 'Oh my lovely man', said she, 'you have a big doubt in your heart about me. How could you say such a thing to me. Amnt I a loving wife working day and night for you? Is it breaking my heart you'll be?' Well he looked into her lovely big eyes and they full of tears, and he was ashamed. 'I am sorry I asked', said he. 'I knew there was no truth in the rumours, oh my love.' He took her in his arms, the dinner went cold and need I say more.

Well things should have been left at that, but that is never the way of the world. The other man still called, the lovely woman was happy and a wonderful woman she was indeed for in the evening time she would have a dinner fit for a king waiting for Joseph and she was a most loving wife. Well things went on satisfactorily for a time and then the rumours began again. This time the husband got really angry and he decided to end the talk once and for all.

He headed home early one afternoon and, God bless the man who invented gravel. They heard the sound of his feet crunching up the pathway. He very nearly caught the other man with his wife. Quick as a flash she ushered the man friend out the window, looked wildly around the kitchen then grabbed a towel which she threw about her shoulders and proceeded to wet her hair in the basin. When her husband opened the door he found her in her skimpy shift, washing her hair in the basin. 'Oh my love', said she, 'I haven't the dinner ready yet, I wasn't expecting you so early'. He looked at her with her damp hair clinging in around her lovely face and the grand white shoulders of her and his heart turned over with love.

What could he do? 'Oh Aisling, Aisling', says he, 'I had to come home because I heard the rumours going the rounds again and I was afraid you would hear them yourself and be upset'. Her heart leapt but she held firm. 'Oh my love', said she, 'what will we do? They are really tormenting us. They are jealous, I suppose, because we are so happy', and she slipped into his arms. 'You are right', says he, 'and do you know what I thought of as I came along home to you, couldn't we go to the Hill of Truth and put an end to the whispers once and for all. What do you think?' Well what could she do only pretend to go along with the idea even though her heart nearly stopped with fright. She could smell the burnt flesh already. 'You are right', said she. 'We'll go'.

Oh isn't the mind of a cornered woman marvellous indeed? That night as they lay in bed they talked. 'I know', said Joseph, 'I will take a few days off work and then we can get a loan of two donkeys and make the journey without too much trouble'.

'Donkeys!' said she, 'me on a donkey!' and there was genuine alarm in her voice.

'Na na na, don't worry', said he. 'I will ask the man who owns the donkeys to come with us and they will be nice and quiet for him'.

She sighed resignedly. 'All right', said she, 'we would have to bring someone with us as a witness anyway so it might as well be the donkey man'.

'Yes' agreed her husband, 'he's very well known and respected, people will accept his word as witness'. This agreed he turned over and slept soundly. Aisling lay awake a long time thinking.

Word spread, as it does, and when Aisling passed through the village there were remarks made loudly like, 'Ah do you get a smell of ashes on the wind this morning?' and there would be a skit of laughter following. There was nothing she could say or do, for sometimes in her own terror she believed she too could smell burning on the wind.

The morning came when they had arranged to go with the donkey man and after all sorts of oh-ing and ah-ing the beautiful Aisling was seated on the donkey. 'I am afraid!' said she. 'Don't be frightened', said the donkey man, 'I will help you and everything will be all right'. So off they went and the whole village out to see them off. Some with spite, whispering how he would be coming back a widower, and others with hope that indeed he might for would he not make a grand husband for one of them. Such is the way of the world.

They stopped several times to eat and to give the donkeys a rest, and all the time the husband wondered if he were doing the right thing. Every time they re-mounted the donkeys his wife became more and more fearful. Then just when they were within sight of the Hill of Truth didn't the donkey she was riding give a sudden buck and down she went head over heels onto the wayside, her clothing over her head and she in a heap. Well was there panic? She crying out in hurt and fear and trying to get her clothing down to cover her nakedness, her husband trying to help her and the donkey man trying to calm the donkey.

Well there was no consoling the beautiful woman now. 'It's all your fault', she said to her husband, 'you and your donkeys, now how can I swear that no man has seen beneath my skirts except you when the donkey man has seen everything? I'll be burnt to ashes over you'. She cried as though her heart would break and he was sorry for her. He held her in his arms and told her he believed her no matter if she never held the golden chain which reached from heaven to the top of the hill. He was a foolish man, he said, to be shamed by the rumours. Just then the donkey man interrupted them. 'It would be a terrible disgrace if we went home and herself not after holding the chain' said he, 'Ye would be destroyed entirely'. They both agreed with him and Aisling wailed even louder. 'But wait a minute now, I think I may have the answer to your problem', he said. That donkey man was clever too.

They went up the hill and, sure enough, there was the golden chain which the good God had left down from heaven and it swinging too and fro in the gentle breeze. On the ground beneath there was a circle of ashes and footprints left by previous visitors to the spot. They were frightened now I can tell you. What would happen to Aisling or indeed to any one of them if they took the chain in their hand and spoke an untruth. Well eventually the lovely woman gathered her courage and taking hold of the Chain of Truth, she was startled to find it soft and warm in her hand and for a minute hesitated. Then quickly, she said, 'No man has ever seen beneath my skirts except my dear husband Joseph and Sean, the donkey man.' There was no thunder, no lightening. Praise be to God! She was all right. The three of them went happily back to Portlaw. No one dared question God's Chain of Truth and everyone was happy.

After that the husband went out to work every morning. The wife cleaned and tidied the house, put out the ashes before lunchtime, not to bring the bad luck, scrubbed off the front step and prepared a dinner fit for a king. In the afternoon, Sean, the donkey man, called as usual, and by dinner time he was gone and the wife waiting with open arms for her husband. What a woman.

But God wasn't happy that the Chain of Truth could be fooled so he took it back up to heaven and from then on the Hill of Truth became known as The Woman's Hill or *Sliabh na mBan*.

# 15

# PRINCE SIGTRYG &
# KING ALEF'S DAUGHTER

*There are many old tales told around Waterford relating to the early invaders, who swept over the south east and in particular, up along the Suir estuary. This is one of the oldest stories told, not only on this side of the Irish Sea, for it is connected very firmly with that grand country of Wales.*

*The first time I heard it was, indeed, in Wales and I was embarrassed to admit that I had not heard it before and I coming directly over from the very city of Waterford. So I listened and learned.*

In the years when the Danes first raided and settled on the banks of the River Suir, many leaders came and went. Eventually, they established their base in Waterford City, or as they called it, Vaderfjord, which, we were told from a young age, meant Safe Haven. Now it seems that some say it was an old west Norse word '*ram fjord*' or 'windy fjord'. In any case it was, indeed, a safe haven, far enough up the river to be safe from the roughest weather and sheltered by lush green banks and forests of trees, which they could use for boat building or repairing.

The Danes were a mighty seafaring race. They were making attacks all along the Irish coast from the late 700s, and their many attempts to set up home were repelled by the local tribesmen. Eventually they established toeholds on the east coast and

Waterford was one of their great achievements. They built a walled city and settled down to trade and intermarry. Waterford was a Danish city for several hundred years.

During this time, as the story goes, there was a prince in Waterford, and he was the son of a Danish King Ranald. He was called Prince Sigtryg Ranaldsson. He was fair-haired and handsome and a great warrior and when his father arranged a marriage for him with the daughter of King Alef from Cornwall, he was pleased to go along with the arrangement. He was to marry the youngest daughter, Fairest, and she, in turn, was more than happy to be marrying Sigtryg, and to be away from her father's court. As a sign of his good intent, he gave to Fairest a ring fit for someone so beautiful. It was all agreed then and a time was set and Sigtryg went off to make his own arrangements.

King Alef was not very circumspect in his dealings and saw his children as a means to make alliances with his enemies. He was also known to change his mind if the wind blew in the other direction, if you know what I mean. Well, the arrangement was made and the only thing now was to wait for the weather to be right, so that Sigtryg could sail back and the wedding could take place. Princess Fairest waited and waited but there was no sign of her prince coming.

Sigtryg was busy helping his own father King Ranald at home in Waterford. They were under attack from some of the local tribes and every man was needed to fight them off. He too was more than a little put out that he could not chase away across the Irish Sea to claim his bride, but it never crossed his mind that there might be a problem.

But there was a problem. King Alef was hard pressed by a man called the Pictish Giant and his clan. So, without a thought in his head for his young daughter, and knowing well that Sigtryg was busy over in Waterford, he promised his daughter in marriage to the Pictish Giant instead. Well she was distraught and begged and pleaded with her father to let her marry Sigtryg, but he would not listen.

Now, as my mother used to say, bless her, the Lord works in mysterious ways. In this case it came in the shape of a famous warrior known as Hereward the Wake. They said he was son of

Earl Leofric of Mercia, which was over on the fenland of the east coast of England. He came into the palace of King Alef on a visit. Straight away Hereward saw that the young Princess Fairest was in distress and besides, he took an instant dislike to the Pictish Giant. He was really only about 8 feet tall but, at that time it was thought to be a huge size.

When Hereward talked with the princess he could see that she wanted to be free of this arrangement so that she could marry Sigtryg, in Waterford, and get far away from her father. So, as people often did then, he picked a fight and managed to kill the Pictish Giant. But he could not kill all the Pictish tribe, who were there for the marriage, so when they put pressure on King Alef, he threw Hereward and his man, Martin, into prison.

Hereward was also dismayed to see that the young princess was crying and swearing she would be revenged for the death of the giant. She even insisted on making sure that they were tied up fast before leaving them in the darkest dungeon. He was sitting in the dungeon, saying as much to his manservant, Martin, when, with a grunt, Martin pulled his hands free.

'You are wronging the lady, for did she not give me this knife to cut us free. She had to pretend to grieve so that her father would not be killed by the Picts.'

Well, Hereward was delighted but even when their bonds were loosed, they could not escape from the dungeon, in which they were held. They decided to try and overpower the guard when he next came and they waited. After a long time the rusty door creaked open and just as Hereward was about to strike, he saw that it was the princess herself who came in followed by an old priest.

She turned to Hereward and said, 'Forgive me please for calling for your death but they would have killed us all. In this way, I have claimed you as my victims. There was no other way I could get near you. Now please, can you help me further and take a message to my betrothed, Sigtryg, son of King Ranald of Waterford? Say to him, that I am beset on every side and unless he comes to claim me some other suitor will come and my father will hand me over because he is afraid.'

Hereward was gallant and chivalrous and he said he would go the minute he got free. The princess insisted that he would tie up herself and the old priest so that no blame would fall on them or her father. She gave to him her ring, which he was to give to Sigtryg.

They stole away down to the harbour and took ship to Ireland. They sailed up the River Suir and straight to the very door of Reginald's Tower, where they disembarked and entered into the hall of King Ranald. There was a great celebration going on, when Hereward came in, for they had just defeated some wild Irish tribe. Straight away, Prince Sigtryg recognised the noble bearing of this stranger and invited him to his own table. As they drank, Hereward contrived to slip the ring into the young prince's goblet.

When Sigtryg saw the ring he knew, from whom it came. He asked Hereward all sorts of urgent questions. He became very angry when he heard about the Pictish Giant, for at first, Hereward did not tell him he had killed the giant. When it was finally told, Sigtryg went to his father and told him of the betrayal of King Alef. With his father's blessing he took ship, with Hereward, on the very next tide and they went back to rescue the princess.

Now all this took time, for they were dependent on winds and weather, so when they finally came back to Cornwall, the lovely princess was once again betrothed to a wild Cornish leader. Haco was his name and the wedding feast was to be held that very day. Sigtryg sent a troop of forty Danes to King Alef, demanding the fulfilment of the marriage agreement between himself and princess Fairest. He threatened war if this were not done. No answer came back; indeed not one single Dane came back.

Sigtryg and Hereward knew now that they were in terrible trouble, so Hereward dressed himself as a travelling minstrel, and he made his way to the wedding feast. During the music and feasting, he drank a toast to the bride and as he touched her goblet he, once again, contrived to drop in the ring. The minute the princess saw the ring gleaming beneath the wine, she knew help had come.

Later on, when everyone was sleeping, and a lot of them slept where they sat in the hall, the old nurse, who was the constant

companion of the princess, came softly to Hereward. They went to meet with the very sad princess. 'You have come too late', she cried. 'Take word to Sigtryg and tell him this was not my will but my father's planning. Sigtryg is still the love of my heart.'

Hereward looked at her and said, 'But Sigtryg is here, he sent his Danes with word and we have heard nothing.'

It was then they realised that the Danes were held in the dungeons, as prisoners, and they would be taken away by Haco, in the morning, as he claimed them as his prisoners. He intended to take them to a deep ravine and there to blind them and release them where they would probably die, being unable to see their way safe.

What can I tell you? Hereward went straight back to Sigtryg and told him everything. They laid a clever ambush and when Haco came, riding along with his own tribesmen, the prisoners and his new bride, they were waiting.

The bridal procession came like this: first the captured Danish prisoners, bound between two Cornishmen, then came Haco and his downcast bride, followed on by tribesmen of Haco, most of whom were still the worse for wear after a night of celebrations.

Sigtryg and Hereward watched as the prisoners went past, with their guards but Hereward was so furious with Haco and what he intended, that he jumped down upon him and cut off his head. Sigtryg took care of his princess and they got free. The prisoners overpowered their guards and before the sun had moved half an inch in the sky they were all away and down to the ship which Sigtryg owned.

Once again they sailed up the River Suir and this time, standing at the prow, with great joy, stood Sigtryg and the Princess Fairest.

There was great rejoicing in the city for the next few days. Prince Sigtryg and Princess Fairest were married with great pomp and ceremony and Hereward and his man Martin stayed on for some time. Then, despite the pleading of their friends to stay always, Hereward said he must go for it is not good to look into happiness through another man's eyes. I think that meant he was a little in love with the princess too.

As they say in all good tales, they lived as long as was decent and left behind them this story and a strong and beautiful City of Waterford.

# 16

# THE STORY OF
# ST DECLAN IN ARDMORE

*In the county of Waterford we have a very famous saint. St Declan is well
known now as the patron saint of different schools and colleges, but what
is not so well known is the fact that he actually came from Co. Waterford.
He is one of our own and there are many startling tales told about him.
The really nice thing about St Declan is that there are references to him
in many historical documents, down through the centuries. This makes
things much easier for storytellers, like myself, to relax into his story and
to know that the background is real and he was a man of the Deise.*

At the time of his birth, this land of ours was very wild and unruly.
There were a lot of very unchristian things happening between tribes,
who fought each other constantly, and life itself was not valued. In
school, we were told that it was a pagan country but sure we didn't
know much about pagans either, except that they had not heard of
Jesus Christ and that they were to be pitied and converted. Bless us
and save us, wasn't that very small knowledge we gained? Neither
did they tell us that St Declan worked miracles and conversed with
angels. That was probably dangerous ground as well.

Well to get back to my story. They say that St Declan was born up
between Colligan and Cappoquin. His father was a man called Erc
Mac Trein and his mother was called Deithin. She carried him without

any discomfort and was on a visit to her husband's brother, Dobhran, when the child came suddenly into the world. It must have caused more than a little excitement, for it is said that a great blaze of light lit up the sky over the house and many angels were seen as the light reached up to high heaven and back down again, almost like a ladder.

Now, they say that something like that happened when St Brigid was born, as well.

You know, it must have been a time of great change for it was common for people to see angels then. It was, after all, only a few hundred years after the birth of Christ and nobody ever questioned the appearance of angels at that time, but took it as normal. People are talking a lot about seeing and hearing angels now, in our own time, and we definitely know that this is a time of great change.

Nobody is really sure of the date of St Declan's birth but by looking up old manuscripts on the lives of other saints and St Declan's own 'Life' the real experts have come to the conclusion that he must have been born in the late 300s or very early 400s.

The holy man who blessed him at his birth was named Coleman and later he became St Coleman. When St Coleman saw the baby he recognised in him the gift of sanctity and holiness and having converted both parents he baptised him and the name given to him was Declan. He impressed on the parents that Declan was one of God's own and that they should ensure he was well taken care of and educated by the very best tutors available. I suppose they were shocked, the *craturs*, by all that had happened on the night of the birth, but they just carried on and did their best for their child, just as any other parent. Some say, that little miracles were always happening around Declan in his youth but that the child never noticed except that God looked after him. He was fostered by his father's brother, Dobhran, as was often the custom then. Dobhran loved his nephew and delighted in his innocent and trusting nature. Declan spent seven years with him being educated, and then the time came when he had to leave Dobhran and his parents and friends and under St Coleman's direction he was sent to a very holy man called Dioma who had studied abroad. Dioma had a monk's cell and Declan and other young men came to learn from him.

There were many disciplines to be studied and Declan loved the path he was following so he had no trouble learning. It took a long time to satisfy his hunger for knowledge and he was with Dioma for many years. During this time, without ever looking for it, Declan began to attract others of like mind. They started to depend on him for direction and he thought it better that he should go to Rome and get proper permission to teach the faith, from the Pope.

Declan and his followers set out for Rome. Their ship would have been a sailing craft and probably had to be rowed as well. That is how ships were then. I don't know what direction they went but it would have been easy enough to cross over to Gaul, as France was called at the time, and then journey by land to Italy. Maybe that is what they did. It would have taken them a very long time.

When they finally arrived in Rome they were met by a holy bishop known as Ailbe. He was working for Pope Hilary, but he knew all about Declan already. He was very good to Declan and his followers and acted as a mentor for him. It seems that Declan conducted himself with dignity and honour and impressed many. After a good while in Rome, Declan was ordained bishop by the Pope, who gave him everything he needed to further his preaching and conversions at home, in Ireland. He got holy books and a set of rules to work by.

Now it seems that during all his travels and his time in Rome, Declan was still instrumental in miraculous healing and cures. It must have been so, for when he set out for home, with the blessing of the Pope ringing in his ears, many Romans decided to follow him including Runan, the son of the king of Rome. I often wondered if there were any who did not like Declan.

Travelling back home on his journey Declan met Patrick who was following his own path in the faith. They must have talked much about the conversions they hoped to make in Ireland and the difficulties they faced. They parted as friends and so it remained all their lives. Two holy men about God's work.

Up to this time all we get is reports of miracles happening but nobody has been in any way specific. But now, on the way back home from Rome a strange thing happened. Declan was beginning mass, one day, when there was sent to him from heaven a little black bell, which came in through the window of the church and remained on the altar before Declan. Declan greatly rejoiced and gave thanks and glory to Christ. It filled him with much courage for what lay ahead. He gave the bell to Runan to carry and keep safe for him. The name his Irish followers put on it was '*The Duibhin Decláin*'. He probably had his hands full himself with all of them following along.

When they finally came to the sea, in northern Gaul, they had not enough money between them to take ship onward. In the end Declan took the sacred bell and striking it he prayed to God for help. Shortly after, they saw coming over the waves towards them an empty, sail-less ship and no one guiding it. As any good Deise man would do, he told his followers to get aboard at once and that it would take them to wherever they were meant to go. Once Declan boarded, with his followers, the boat took them safely across the sea to England. When they stepped ashore the ship turned and went on its way again. Lord only knows what business they had to do there but some say that they came into Wales and met with St David. There was certainly a *flúirse* of saints around that time.

Now we come to the next strange thing. When they finally set out for Ireland didn't Runan give the little holy bell, belonging to Declan, to one of the others to mind while they were loading up their belongings for the trip. I suppose they were all doing their best but the one minding the little holy bell set it down out of his hand on a rock and forgot all about it. They were halfway across the sea to Ireland when he remembered it.

Well, can you imagine how hard it must have been for them to tell Declan what had happened. He was a good man and didn't blame anyone even though he probably did feel a bit sad at losing the holy bell. He decided to talk to God and ask if the bell could come to him again. Trusting completely, he told his followers not to worry and within a short while one of them called out and there, following their little craft, was the rock on which the bell had been

left and there upon it was the little holy bell. All on board the boat gave glory to God. Declan told them to permit the bell to lead them and to follow it exactly to where ever it would come to rest. There he told them he would set up his city and his bishopric and there he would stay, until he returned to paradise.

They followed the rock, carrying the holy bell, until it stopped at a small island off the south coast of Munster. Declan went ashore and gave thanks to God. The story goes that one of his followers asked Declan 'How can this "little height" support your people?' And Declan replied 'Do not call it little hill, beloved son, but "great height",' and that name has been on the area ever since – *Ardmore – Decláin*.

The island belonged to the Deise and Declan, being once again near home, set out to ask the Deise king for the island. Declan's miracles were well known in the area and the king gave him the island for his church. When Declan came back his followers were concerned that they would find it difficult to go back and forth to the mainland and that the people would not be able to get out to Declan's church, if the weather turned rough.

Declan thought about it and said this is the place God has sent us to. So they talked some more and it was decided that Declan would ask God to help and taking his bishop's crozier he went down to the shore. Declan must have felt under a lot of pressure and a bit uncomfortable with what he now had to do.

They prayed a lot first, then Declan, taking the crozier in his hand, struck the water in the name of the Father and of the Son and of the Holy Ghost and made the sign of the cross over the water and immediately, by command and permission of God, the sea commenced to move out from its place. It happened so quickly that many fish were left stranded and Declan, still holding his crozier, followed the sea as it went out away from the land around the island until it was an island no more.

Well with that problem solved, Declan and his followers began to build a great monastery. They called it *Ardmore Decláin*. It was a place of great learning and healing as Declan continued to work miracles, by the grace of God, whenever the need arose.

Declan, by his living example of peaceful and gentle ways, drew many people to him, and these were trained in Christianity and helped to spread the faith in many places. Churches were built and whole clans converted before the arrival of St Patrick. (He had been held up a long while in Rome and had differences with his own superiors in England.) So when St Patrick arrived in Ireland, Declan and the other bishops, already there, had done a great deal of work.

St Patrick blazed his own trail of miracles and he was in Cashel when he heard that one of the princes of the Deise was not accepting Declan's teaching so he decided to speak with the prince himself. But the prince would not have anything to do with Christianity and so it was that the Angel of Peace came to Declan and told him to hurry to meet with St Patrick as he was praying against the man of the Deise and the whole clan would be cursed if he didn't get there in time. Declan took off as speedily as possibly and went over Sliabh gCua and crossed the River Suir and came to where St Patrick was. He asked St Patrick not to curse the people. St Patrick said that he would not curse them because Declan had asked and instead he would give them a blessing.

Declan went one last time to try and change the mind of the king of the Deise but that man would not be swayed even though all his people were now baptised; he wanted to hold to the old ways. Then Declan turned to the people and told them to separate themselves from this man lest they be cursed on his account. The people listened to Declan and no longer accepted the king. In his place Declan encouraged them to accept Feargal MacCormac, who was a good young man and the people gladly did so.

In the years left to St Declan it is said that many miracles took place by God's grace and many young men were educated to spread the Christian faith. When his years in this life were drawing to a close St Declan requested that he be attended by a disciple of his own, MacLaig. His last hours were spent in the company of his own people and he blessed them before he passed to his final reward. The little place near the sea where he liked to spend time in peace and prayer is still a place of pilgrimage and there stands a holy well where prayers are said to St Declan for cures. His feast day is celebrated on 24 July.

# 17

# St Declan's Miracles

*St Declan had a huge influence on the lives of the people of Co. Waterford. Everywhere you turn there is a school or a church or a parish dedicated to his memory. It is no wonder then that there are many stories still firmly entrenched in local history and folklore. If all the stories are to be believed, then he was truly a genuine saint of the people and a miracle worker of God.*

There is a story about St Declan which is a cause of wonder. It appears that the castle of the King of the Deise caught fire and was in danger of being completely destroyed. When all hope of saving it seemed lost, St Declan came along the way, and from about a mile distant he saw the castle burning. He was upset and in that instant he flung his staff and it flew through the air until it reached the centre of the flames and they were immediately extinguished. The king and all those present gave praise to God and Declan for saving the castle. The king's castle was near the River Suir and the place from which Declan threw his staff was known as Mag Laca in ancient times.

Another time, it is told, St Patrick sent one of his own followers, Ballin, to visit St Declan and the poor man was almost at the end of his journey when he drowned while crossing a river, not far from

Ardmore. When St Declan heard of this he was in an awful state. What would he say to St Patrick?

He got into his chariot, by all accounts, and headed straight towards the place where the tragedy had occurred. By the time that he reached them the people had pulled the follower of St Patrick from the water and were carrying him on a bier. St Declan asked them to rest it a while until he prayed over the poor drowned man. They did what he asked and waited patiently.

St Declan began to talk to God and then he commanded 'In the name of the Trinity, in the name of the Father and of the Son and of the Holy Ghost whose religious yoke I bear myself, arise to us, for God has given your life to me.' Straight away the man came back to himself and greeted St Declan. He stayed with Declan for some time as he was not yet fully recovered. When he finally returned to St Patrick and told him how St Declan had raised him from the dead, St Patrick and his followers all praised God for the miracle he had worked through St Declan.

Sliabh gCua is famous in song and story but one of the more interesting miracles of St Declan occurred while crossing over Sliabh gCua. The horse, which was drawing his chariot, fell lame and he was unable to carry on with this journey until he saw some deer nearby. He took the halter from the horse and handed it to one of his followers and sent him over to the herd of wild deer, telling him to bring one of the deer to pull the chariot. His man, knowing Declan well by now, did what he was told and approached the largest and strongest deer in the herd. He placed the halter on him and brought him back where the deer willingly allowed himself to be yoked to the chariot of the saint. He drew the chariot along to the destination the saint wished to reach and then, with a blessing, St Declan released the deer to return to its own life.

In the time of St Declan there were many dangers to monasteries and the townships around them. Not least, was the risk of pirates or invaders from the sea who liked to plunder any place they could, for gold and treasure or indeed for cattle and people as slaves. Now Ardmore, which was called St Declan's city and monastery, was the

target of one such raid. Seeing the approaching raiders it is said that the people called on St Declan to ask God to save them.

St Declan called one of his strong young followers, whose name was Ultan, and he sent him down to the shore to face the approaching raiders. Ultan stood on the shore and prayed to God as Declan had instructed. Then he held out his left hand against them and didn't the sea swallow them up. The story is that they were turned into great lumps of rock and that these rocks are there, at the entrance to the bay to this very day. An old saying in this area, in times of danger, was, 'The left hand of Ultan against you'.

These and many more stories are told about St Declan and so it is no wonder that even today people make pilgrimage to Ardmore to see for themselves the site where the holy man spent his days.

If you journey to Ardmore you can see what remains of his monastery. There under the shadow of a later edifice, the famous eleventh-century round tower, you can see the ruins of his cathedral with the famous panels of biblical scenes on the external west gable. Even though they are weather-beaten with the passing years they can still be photographed successfully.

St Declan is said to be buried in the area known as The Beannachán. Many people, down the years, have taken away handfuls of clay from this grave site as it is said to cure many ailments.

The Holy Well of St Declan remains accessible to all; if you walk up from the beach and go past the Cliff Hotel you will find the well near the ruins of what is said to have been the 'quiet place' that the saint retired to and spent his last years.

The pattern day for St Declan is 24 July.

# 18

# 'RIANN BÓ PHADRAIG'

*If you look at the map of the mountains of Co. Waterford, you will see plainly that some of the Knockmealdown Mountains are indeed inside the boundaries of Co. Waterford. There is a story, which has been handed down through the generations, about a track over these mountains. Many strange happenings seem to have occurred when all the saints, God bless them all, were alive and well in young Ireland. The tale that is told is as follows.*

St Patrick had a cow which had a calf. This would not have been strange at all then, for there was a tradition that saints and holy men were given cows and hens and the like so that they would have their own supply of the very essentials for survival.

Now St Patrick's cow must have been a very special cow, and what else would you expect and she owned by a saint. When her calf was stolen away by a rogue from Co. Waterford, who crossed the Knockmealdown Mountains to rustle away the holy cow's calf, didn't she get herself into an awful rage and go tearing after him. In her anger and distress, it is said (and who am I to dispute it?) that by dint of her trampling hooves and gouging horns didn't she wear a wide strip of a pathway over the mountains and down into Co. Waterford, where she caught up with the calf rustler and,

having dealt with him in her own fashion, she took her calf back over the mountains to be with St Patrick, in the safety of Cashel.

The route she took on that fateful day was thereafter to be known as '*Riann Bó Phadraig*', or 'The Track of St Patrick's Cow'. Some parts of this route are still traceable to this very day, and it is said to be a continuation of the walk known as St Declan's Way, which stretched from Ardmore to Lismore.

# 19

# LITTLE NELLIE
# OF HOLY GOD

*Did you know that Little Nellie of Holy God was born in Waterford?*
*I remember hearing about this holy child when I was in school but for*
*some reason I didn't realise that she was one of our own.*

*Little Nellie of Holy God was born in the Military Barracks, in*
*Waterford on 24 August 1903. Her father was William Organ,*
*from Dungarvan, and her mother was Mary Aherne, from Portlaw.*
*Wouldn't you think we would be more aware of her story here in*
*Waterford, instead of letting Cork take all the credit for her?*

She was born into a family with three other children, Thomas,
David and Mary. It was in old Ballybricken Church that she was
baptised Ellen Organ and Nellie became her pet name in the
family. She was tiny, bless her, and they all loved her.

The world she was born into was filled with conflict and Waterford
was an occupied city. The choices people had were limited, if they
wished to survive. Her father had been unable to find work to
support his little family and so the only choices left to him were emigration or joining up with the British Army. By this time his wife,
Mary, was unwell, so emigration was not a choice he could make.

He must have been heart scalded to do it, but he enlisted in the
Royal Infantry Barracks, Waterford, in October 1897. They were

given accommodation in the married quarters attached to the barracks and it was there, six years later that little Nellie was born.

Joining the regiment in Waterford did not mean that William Organ would be left in Waterford permanently. The nature of soldiering is movement and so in 1905 he was transferred, with the Royal Artillery, to Spike Island in Cork. His little family had to up sticks and move with him.

Little Nellie was always fascinated by her mother's rosary beads and the prayers to Holy God. Her father remembered her at this time, as toddling along beside him, holding his hand and talking about Holy God.

The health of Mary began to deteriorate and it was evident that she had tuberculosis. TB was at epidemic proportions throughout Ireland at that time and I recall my mother pointing out a house to us, over the Ferry Road, where a whole family died within weeks of each other. She used to bless herself and make us do the same when we passed.

Little Nellie was only four the year her mother passed away in the January of 1907. There was little help or pity then for bereaved families of military men and her father found it impossible to care for his children, as well as fulfilling his military duties.

For a time he got help from kind neighbours but soon it became evident that this was not working out to benefit of the children. Little Nellie cried a lot and missed her mother more so than the older children. She had been in the habit of staying close to her mother and her little way of talking to Holy God as she played with her mother's rosary beads, was gone from her.

Although it distressed him greatly, William Organ decided that the only and best course of action he could take was to place his children in care. Nellie and her sister Mary were placed with the Good Shepherd Sisters at their Industrial School, St Finbar's, in Sunday's Well, Cork.

The two boys Thomas and David were settled in at different locations. Sure wasn't that a cruelty in itself, separating the poor little children from each other? Thomas was sent to the School of the Brothers of Charity at Upton and David to the Convent School of

the Sisters of Mercy in Passage West. I often wonder if the adults at that time had any pity or understanding of children at all.

In any case Little Nellie and her sister Mary settled into their life with the nuns. Both little girls were sick with whooping cough when they arrived and it was discovered that the cause of Little Nellie's misery was the fact that her back and hips had been injured in a fall as a baby, and had never been seen to or recognised, even until then. The poor little child must have been in terrible pain for a long time. Did the four children ever get to see each other again? You can't help but wonder.

She loved the nuns and called them 'Mothers'. She is reported to have said to Ms Hall, who nursed her, that Holy God took her mother and gave her another 'Mother' to mind her. Even though she was only an infant, she knew all about Holy God and the nuns were amazed to hear her talk. Because of her back and hip injuries she found it hard to walk without help and spent a lot of time in her cot.

The nuns had set up a little altar in the room near her, with a Child of Prague statue and some flowers. Little Nellie loved this and looked on the statue as her 'baby'. She would cuddle the statue to her and spend a long time talking to Holy God. She startled those who took care of her, more than once, by reporting that 'Him' was dancing for her and she would ask that they make music, so 'Him' could dance for her. The fact that they could not see what was clearly visible to her made no difference. Her little face would light up with joy and seem to shine brightly as she engaged with her Holy God.

She persuaded the nuns to bring her to the chapel when the Blessed Sacrament was taken out of the Tabernacle and put on Exposition. On the first occasion she became very animated, calling out 'There He is!' After that she always knew, without being told, that Holy God was not, as she said 'in the lock-up' in His house. Those who looked after her were happy to carry her down to the chapel to see her Holy God.

Another startling fact became apparent as the time passed. She could tell if those attending her had received the Blessed Sacrament. She would always ask why they did not get Holy God into their hearts. One of those who attended her regularly, Mary Long, reported that if she pretended that she had received the Sacrament then Little Nellie would say to her that she had not done so. There was no deceiving the little innocent child. Her health was getting progressively worse but she never complained.

It was discovered now that she suffered from caries and that the bone of her jaw was rotting away. The child must have been in mortal agony. She would cling tightly to her Rosary beads and lie very still when the pain was bad. I do not know what medication would have been available then and I understand the doctor and those who nursed her were filled with pity but she would have none of it. Someone had told her the story of Jesus and her understanding and empathy with the crucified Jesus made her cry. She would often say that poor Holy God suffered more than her on His cross.

Around this time her health was very poor and she was given the sacrament of Confirmation by the Bishop of Cork. She was still only four years old. People were often confirmed, long ago, if it was believed they were going to die. It was to give them strength and often did.

Her constant request, in the last months of her little life, was for Holy God to come to her through receiving Holy Communion. She became so desperate to have Holy God in her heart that she begged the nuns to come straight up to her after they received Holy Communion and to kiss her, so she could be near to Holy God. Bless them, they did this for the child.

A Jesuit priest was giving a retreat to the nuns when he heard about Little Nellie and her love of Holy God and her wish for Holy Communion. He dropped what he was doing and went straight away to visit with her. He was astounded, at her childish understanding of God and the absolute love and trust she had in her Holy God.

He reported to the Bishop of Cork and explained about Little Nellie and her devotion to Holy God and the condition of her health. The bishop agreed immediately that Little Nellie could receive the Blessed Sacrament, even though children then did not receive the sacrament until they were twelve years of age.

It is said that when Little Nellie heard the great news that she was beside herself with joy and went into a state of ecstasy. She insisted that she be dressed all in white and with flowers in her hair for the special event. She loved fresh flowers and would often tell the nuns to take away the 'bad' flowers and to get fresh ones, for Holy God.

The day she received her First Holy Communion was a day of wonder to many. Everyone gathered to be with Little Nellie, as they knew she was longing for this more than anything in the world. She went into a state of high spirituality and it was reported that a glowing light surrounded her. Many hours afterwards she was still in communion with Holy God.

Immediately after she received the Blessed Sacrament it is reported that the terrible smell which had come from the rotted jaw bone vanished. Little Nellie seemed to improve in her health for a small while and was well enough to be taken out to the garden.

But, she too had developed tuberculosis, like her poor mother before her, and it was only a matter of time until she reached her last days. She constantly talked with Holy God now and the nuns, recognising that she was a special child of God, spent as much time with her as possible. There are many reports of the little girl giving messages, to those about her, which came to them from Holy God. On one occasion, a nun wanted to know if Holy God would soon take her too, only to be told that 'Him' said she had to get better and do what Holy God wanted of her first. This nun lived to a ripe old age and hopefully fulfilled her mission in this world.

In the last weeks of her life, Little Nellie was very poorly but never complained. On the day she went to meet her Holy God finally she was peaceful and seemed to be in silent conversation with someone near the end of her bed. Her eyes then gazed upwards and with a smile on her face she passed over.

Little Nellie of Holy God died on Sunday, 2 February 1908. She had lived for four years, five months and eight days.

She was buried, at first, in St Joseph's Cemetery in Cork but a year and a half later permission was sought and obtained to have her remains transferred to the Good Shepherd Convent Cemetery. When her little remains were taken up it was discovered that her body was incorrupt and there was no sign of the disease which had caused her so much pain.

Many pilgrims still visit the grave of Little Nellie of Holy God in the Convent Cemetery and people have claimed healing through her intercession.

Pope Pious X was very impressed with the story of Little Nellie and as a direct result of hearing about her little holy life he made a ruling which permitted children to receive the Blessed Sacrament at a much younger age.

# 20

# MOUNT
# MELLERAY

Mount Melleray Abbey is a community of Cistercian (Trappist) monks. The monastery is situated on the slopes of the Knockmealdown Mountains in Co. Waterford, Ireland.

There was a Melleray Abbey in Brittany – originally a twelfth-century foundation – and it was from this community that the Cistercians who came to Ireland were descended. The French Abbey was closed down more than once due to political upheaval and in 1830 those who remained in the Melleray Abbey in Brittany were once again scattered. The French monks were sent to jail and the Irish and English monks were sent back to Ireland. According to the 'History' of Mount Melleray, they were sent aboard a French Battleship, *Hebé*.

The land, on which Mount Melleray stands, just outside Cappoquin in Co. Waterford, was originally described as an extensive wild waste plateau of un-reclaimed mountain land, known as '*Scrahan*', or rough, barren place.

Many such places still exist in Waterford to the present day, but no one would consider building on them. The Cistercian monks who received the grant of this land, from Sir Richard Keane, were more than grateful for his donation. They had nowhere else to go, having searched high and low, and it was only through the good graces of a priest, Revd P. Fogarty, Catholic Curate of Dungarvan, who was a friend to Prior Dom Vincent, that Sir Richard, kindly gave them the land.

On 30 May 1832 Dom Vincent and a friend took possession of this site. As for accommodation the only building on the whole site was an old cottage, containing two small rooms and a kitchen. Even this was like paradise to the good man for he was heart-sore and weary, traipsing the country for a place to start his little monastery. Sure, weren't they great holy men?

The country then was in a terrible state of disruption, so it was a courageous act to set up a monastery at all. We were occupied, as usual, by the invading English and the Tithe Wars were on-going. The poorest people were expected to pay beyond their means and landholders began to withhold their tithes to the Church of Ireland, which really was the British Crown. The Yeomen were seizing property at the slightest chance and there were reprisals being made against them. Perhaps the site up on the side of the mountain was not a bad choice after all. There was nothing there that any Yeoman would want.

The local people, though their own possessions were few enough, gave to Dom Vincent, some chairs, a table and a bed. His delight was great, and humble though the little cottage was, he decided to name it Bethlehem, because it was the birthplace of the religious life of Mount Melleray. Wasn't that a grand idea?

The following day, 31 May, he consecrated his new residence and celebrated Holy Mass for the first time within its walls. In the days, weeks and months that followed he was often joined by the local people as well as those who came from afar and they worked constantly on the clearing of the site. The times that they were in, with people being put out of their homes and no work, meant that often poor people would come and help with the work and get fed, in exchange for their labour. Because it was so high up it must have been a cold windy place, with little shelter, in the early years.

It was back-breaking work and all done by manual labour. Sure they were lucky to even have the tools to do that. The shifting of great lumps of rock and stone, and the clearing of rush and

scrub, proceeded slowly. However, by the following year, 1833, they had enough space cleared for Sir Richard Keane to lay the cornerstone for the new monastery. It was a great day of celebration for the monks and local people and was attended by the Bishop of the diocese.

Mount Melleray, the monastery, was taking shape. More holy men had joined the little community now and constant labouring to clear and reclaim the site went on. They needed to be self-sufficient in every way, so land had to be made ready for planting and sowing. Animals and fowl would have to be acquired, housed and fed. Beside that they would need to plant vegetables and fruit to support themselves. It was a daunting project but one which, with God's help, would be possible.

It was with great joy that Dom Vincent, in the year 1835, saw his little monastery created an abbey. He was unanimously elected and received the Abbatial Blessing from Dr Abraham, Bishop of the diocese. His was the first Abbatial Blessing in Ireland since the Protestant Reformation. With his enthusiasm for the whole venture renewed, he threw himself into all the necessary work of running an Abbey. Part of his work included the founding of a little school for those who came to join the Cistercian Order. He wore himself out, the poor man, and ten years later he passed to his eternal reward.

Well, the abbot who came after him found it very hard going and resigned after two years. The next abbot devoted his energies to expanding the little school into an Ecclesiastical Seminary and sending out missionaries to different places, in Ireland and abroad. It was nearly ninety years later when the building work was resumed in Mount Melleray.

The new abbot, at that time, was Dom Marius O'Phelan, and he decided to continue with the building work and was fortunate in being able to secure a huge supply of limestone blocks from Mitchelstown Castle. The castle was approximately 28 miles west of Mount Melleray and had been burnt by the local IRA in August 1922. Isn't it a true saying, that it is an ill wind that does not blow some good?

The owners of Mitchelstown Castle dismantled the ruins in 1925 and the stones were transported by steam lorry to Mount Melleray. It was a huge task and by all accounts it took two consignments a day for at least five years. Isn't that hard to imagine? All that loading and transporting and then unloading again, for five whole years. There must have been many an aching back and the not so holy words, when a stone slipped or slid the wrong way. The stones were laid out in the fields in preparation for the actual building of the monastery. The plans had to be drawn up carefully, for this building was intended to last a long time, and so it has, thanks be to God.

When Dom Marius died he was succeeded by Dom Celsus O'Connell, who continued to build. He decided to build on the more prominent site directly over the remains of 180 of his fellow Cistercians. I am sure they had no objections as their blood, sweat and tears had gone into the setting up and building the monastery.

Mount Melleray Abbey became a place of learning, peace and healing. Ordinary people found a welcome and were given advice and shelter. The lands around the buildings became fertile and well cared for, producing everything the monks needed. The farmlands were cultivated and herds taken care of by the monks.

As the years sped by the Cistercian monks of Mount Melleray continued their prayer-filled lives, as missionaries and spiritual teachers. Their lifestyle has sometimes drawn many to their community in Co. Waterford and at other times they have struggled with a lack of vocations. Always they have had an open door for any who called, whether they had a vocation or not. They have a guesthouse now where people can come and stay, to find peace of mind and body. They are a listening ear in times of trouble and sorrow and have inspired many to walk their own paths with renewed spirit and joy.

The grounds there have beautiful walks and you can join with the monks in prayer, if you so desire. It has come a long way from a barren, rock-strewn hillside. Sir Richard Keane must hold a high seat in heaven for his kindness to the monks of Mount Melleray, on that first day when he gave them this site.

## THE GROTTO

A statue of the Blessed Virgin is situated at Our Lady of Lourdes Grotto, a little bit away from Mount Melleray Abbey and this has been a place of pilgrimage since it was first set in place. A clear spring of water bubbles out from a little well at the shrine and people come from all over to pray and take home some of the holy water.

In 1985 Ireland was hit by the phenomenon of the Moving Statues and the grotto in Melleray became part of this sensation. The visions at Melleray were reported by three children, Ursula O'Rourke (seventeen), Tom Cliffe (twelve) and Barry Buckley (eleven). There were reports, daily, of visions and the Blessed Virgin moving at the grotto.

Religious fervour brought hundreds of people to Melleray and the Rosary was recited publicly and many claimed that they heard the Holy Mother speak to them. This took place at the Grotto in Melleray between 18 August and 23 August 1985.

There were reports also of the sun dancing in the sky and if the newspapers are to be believed some people reported miraculous cures, but no official confirmation of any of these events is available.

The Catholic Church did not become involved in any of this and quietly distanced itself from the event.

## OGHAM STONES

Within the monastery itself you will find traces of a more ancient Ireland for they have included, in a beautiful courtyard, five Ogham stones. They did not come from the Melleray site but were brought there in 1910 from a place called Kilgrovan in Ballinacourty by Revd Canon P. Power who had a passion for archaeology. The five *Ogham* stones are displayed as part of and exhibition called Buaille na gCuimhnte (Courtyard of Memories).

# 21

# MASTER McGRATH

Did you ever notice the way dogs affect people? We always had a dog in our house when we were growing up. We lived in the country and my Dad, God be good to him, loved nothing better than to be away through the fields with the dog. He would often talk to us about how dogs were different. In fact, sometimes he seemed to imply that they were just like people, some nice and gentle, some fierce and strong, and others outstanding animals altogether.

Master McGrath was one of the outstanding animals. He was a greyhound and sometimes when my Dad talked about greyhounds we got the notion that they were not to be trifled with. A man's greyhound is part of his livelihood, he would say. If you ever harm a greyhound you could end up in jail. We used to shiver at that. How he thought a bunch of little girls might harm a greyhound I don't know.

Well to cut a long story short, he used to tell us about the great Master McGrath and how this wonderful animal was born a small, weak pup in a litter of seven little greyhounds. Sure couldn't we see him, in our mind's eye, cuddled up with his brothers and sisters, snug and safe? He was mostly black with white markings and he would always be small, for a greyhound. The place he came into the world was indeed safe, for a grey-

MASTER M GRATH

hound; it was up beyond Dungarvan in the Co. Waterford. He was born at Colligan Lodge in the year 1866. The man who bred and trained the greyhounds there was called James Galwey and he was well known all over the land as a good trainer and owner of greyhounds.

Master McGrath was not the name he was called as a pup. No, he was called 'Dicksy' and even though he was small, he was strong, in his own way, as he survived where another weaker pup might have given up and perished. Other than that determination to live and get strong he didn't display any outstanding qualities that might mark him as special.

He was not great when it came to training and he was showing so poorly and didn't seem interested in chasing the hare, that his owner decided he would be best given away to someone who was not so interested in breeding winners. But little 'Dicksy' had won the heart of his handler who would have been called his 'slipper'. That was the name of the lad who would let him off at the traps to chase the hare.

Well this lad took charge of him and worked away with him. He believed in the little pup, you see. When he was old enough he entered him in several races and believe it or not didn't he start to win? Once that started to happen wasn't his trainer, James Galwey, very interested in him again and the lucky little pup was returned to him?

Now greyhound racing is a very serious business and a lot of work went into getting him ready for his first big race. He was loaded up and taken, with other dogs, over to England for the great race known as The Waterloo Cup.

Even though James Galwey was his trainer, his real owner was Lord Lurgan and you can imagine his delight when his greyhound bounded clear of the field to win the cup. He was especially proud of his dog because his fellow lords and ladies had laughed at him for entering him in the great race, in the first instance. The more they put bets against him the more Lord Lurgan put for him to win.

Now, you will agree, any greyhound might win the Waterloo Cup once but little 'Dicksy', who was now called Master McGrath, after the lad who trained him, came in as winner on three occasions. He won in 1868, 1869 and 1871 and he was the first greyhound to do that. That little dog had great heart. He was famous all over the racing world and people put bets on him, whenever he was racing, and invariably won lots of money. Lord Lurgan had a lot of money on him and he won so much that he was able to build a full terrace of houses in Walthamstow. It was called Master McGrath Terrace. Sure he must have been rolling in money from the little greyhound's efforts.

Now, you are probably wondering what happened in 1870. He was entered that year too but it was a frosty and icy course and didn't the *cratur* fall through ice and into a river called the Alt. He was saved by one of the Irish lads, named Wilson, who went in to the water and got him out. Sure, it could have been the end of both of them. Lord Lurgan got such a fright he said he might never race him again. But pride and belief in Master McGrath took him back the following year and he rejoiced to see the little greyhound with the mighty heart speed to victory once again.

When he won the Waterloo Cup for the third time Lord Lurgan got a message that the Queen, who was the famous Queen Victoria, would like to see Master McGrath. Can you imagine that? The Queen and the Royal Family wanted to meet with Lord Lurgan and Master McGrath. I bet he was groomed up to the nines for his meeting with the Queen. The Royal Family have always had an interest in dogs and indeed it is reported that Queen Victoria and Prince Albert, her husband, had a black and white pet greyhound themselves, so I suppose it was not that strange except that Master McGrath was from our own place in Colligan, Co. Waterford.

He went from being given away to becoming the most famous greyhound in the world. The lad who had minded him and kept him, when no one else had faith in him, young McGrath, must have been proud to bursting. Wasn't it a grand thing they did calling the dog after the lad who believed in him?

You know that dogs have lives much shorter than our own, bless them. Well, after winning for the third time it was decided that he had raced enough and I suppose they didn't want to break his luck. They kept him instead to be a sire to many more pups. He didn't last too long after his last win. Two years later, in 1873, he died. They said he had a heart that was twice the size of a normal dog's heart and it just gave out. He was buried in the grounds of a house called 'Solitude' in Lurgan.

He was so famous and the people were so proud of his achievements that they did something wonderful, which had never happened before; they erected a monument to him in Co. Waterford near where he was born. If you want to see it for yourself just go through Dungarvan and at the junction of the Clonmel and Cappoquin Road there it stands in all its glory.

There was a ballad composed to commemorate his great wins at the Waterloo Cup.

Eighteen sixty eight being the date and the year,
Those Waterloo sportsmen and more did appear;
For to gain the great prizes and bear them away',
Never counting on Ireland and Master McGrath.

On the twelfth of December, that day of renown,
McGrath and his keeper they left Lurgan town;
A gale in the Channel, it soon drove them o're,
On the thirteenth they landed on fair England's shore.

And when they arrived there in big London town,
Those great English sportsmen all gathered round –
And one of the gentlemen gave a 'Ha! Ha!' saying,
'Is that the great dog you call Master McGrath?'

And one of those gentlemen standing around
Says, 'I don't care a damn for your Irish greyhound,'
And another he laughs with a scornful 'Ha! Ha!
We'll soon humble the pride of your Master McGrath.'

Then Lord Lurgan stepped forward and said, 'Gentlemen,
If there's any among you has money to spend –
For your grand English nobles I don't care a straw –
Here's five thousand to one upon Master McGrath.'

Then McGrath he looked up and he wagged his old tail,
Informing his lordship, 'I know what you mane,
Don't fear, noble Brownlow, don't fear them, agra,
For I'll tarnish their laurels,' says Master McGrath.

And Rose stood uncovered, the great English pride,
Her master and keeper were close by her side;
They have let her away and the crowd cried 'Hurrah!',
For the pride of all England – and Master McGrath.

And Rose and the Master they both ran along,
'Now I wonder,' says Rose, 'what took you from your home;
You should have stayed there on your Irish domain,
And not come to gain laurels on Albion's plain.'

'Well, I know,' says McGrath, 'we have wild heather bogs
But you'll find in old Ireland there's good men and dogs.
Lead on, bold Britannia, give none of your jaw,
Stuff that up your nostrils,' says Master McGrath.

Then the hare she went on just as swift as the wind
He was sometimes before her and sometimes behind.
Rose gave the first turn according to law;
But the second was given by Master McGrath.

The hare she led on with a wonderful view.
And swift as the wind o'er the green field she flew.
But he jumped on her back and he held up his paw
'Three cheers for old Ireland,' says Master McGrath.

I've known many greyhounds that filled me with pride,
In the days that are gone, but it can't be denied,
That the greatest and the bravest that the world ever saw,
Was our champion of champions, great Master McGrath.

*There are many websites with information on Master McGrath and according to Wikipedia there was also a tune; 'The Master McGrath Gallop' by H.R. Callcott, RAM (composer of the* Massereene Waltzes).

# 22

# THE

# SPEAKING STONE

In a small tributary of the River Tay, in the townland of Durrow near Stradbally, stands *An Cloch Labhrais*, probably Ireland's largest glacial erratic boulder. Its name means 'The Speaking Stone', and derives from the tradition that, in ancient times, the stone possessed magical powers of determining whether a person, denying a crime of which he or she had been accused, was telling the truth or not.

But is there no limit to the wiles of the fair sex? One day a woman accused of having committed adultery announced that she would swear to her innocence upon this stone. As the party approached the stone, the woman's lover appeared in the guise of a poor hermit, who humbly offered to carry the woman on his shoulders across the raging torrent to take her oath at the stone. When they had struggled through the stream, the woman laid her hand upon the stone and swore that no man had ever been between her legs, apart from her husband – and of course, the poor hermit who had just carried her there.

Thus the Speaking Stone was forced to declare that she had told the truth, but so enraged was it at such trickery that it cried out in a loud voice: *Bíonn an fhírinne féin searbh* – 'Truth itself is bitter' – and split in two with a crack like thunder. Since

then, not one word has it uttered, in either of the national languages.

Go there and try it out for yourself.

*Main source: Account of Co. Waterford written by Sir Richard Cox, c. 1685. Published in Decies, no. 36 (1987). My thanks to Julian Walton, folklorist for this story.*

# 23

# THE
# FENOR MELEE

In the early 1920s there was a Labourers' strike in Co. Waterford; a lot of it was to do with farm labourers and the state of their lives. Times were very hard then and a great many farmers who took on labourers for seasonal work were probably hard-pressed themselves. There were others who were better off, but all paid only a pittance to the seasonal labourers for desperately long hours and very back-breaking work.

All the work was done by manpower then, with only the threshing machine being a new-fangled thing to help with the saving of the corn. The planting, sowing and reaping and binding were hard work, and men would be seen working with scythes cutting hay and corn. Others would follow on binding the sheaves and making them into little stooks, which would stand all around the fields drying, until the time came when they would be stacked into greater stooks and made secure from the weather, until the farmer was ready to have it milled.

The notion of joining a union was something that was new and strange but at the same time very welcome to the labourers, who had no one to stand up for them. So when the opportunity arose they decided to join the union and small blame to them for they had families to feed and rebellion was in the very air at that time.

This is what happened in Co. Waterford. The local labourers joined the union and demanded better treatment and pay. The farmers were not happy at all with this. It meant they had to deal more fairly with their seasonal workers as well as the permanently employed. They met and promptly decided they would bring in outside help to do the work. Need I tell you now, the labourers were never going to take this lying down, so many an angry word was exchanged until finally, in desperation, some of the farm labourers in the Fenor and Dunhill area decided to take action.

The story goes that they gathered on the road, at Fenor Cross, with the full intention of preventing the threshing machine being used by outside labourers. They were armed with rifles and hurleys and the following song is an account of what happened. This song is still well known and sometimes still rendered in moments of nostalgia in the local public houses.

The month of November being late in the year,
When the Labourers of Fenor they did appear
To uphold the Union best way they should,
And to put down the farmers the best way they could.

At the cross roads of Fenor the machine did appear,
With police in the front and police in the rear.
The driver he came from a place called Kilbride,
And he swore that he'd thrash the police by his side.

On a fine Monday morning with a beautiful sea
With rifles and hurleys and some dressed in green,
To shout 'Up the Labour, no threshing today
And to hell with the farmers we'll burn the hay.'

The machine it did turn and home it did steer,
Both peelers and drives were shaking with fear,
They never looked back 'til they went out of sight
And as fast as the wind they flew home to Kilbride.

Here's to the man down in lower Ballyduff
Kill and Dunhill were both strong and tough,
And the brave men of Fenor their courage they showed,
The day that they stopped the machine on the road.

Long life to Dick Whelan and brave Hanley,
And also Dick Dalton who fought manfully
Although they're in prison, remembered they'll be
For the part that they played in the Fenor Melee.

Now here's the conclusion to finish my song
(I hope you won't say that the verses are wrong),
The farmers of Fenor are shaking with fear
Saying what will we do with corn this year?

# 24

# PICKARDSTOWN AMBUSH 1921

It was a cold winter's night in December and the year was 1920, when a group of young men met secretly to plan an ambush. They came mainly from Waterford City and county, but there were some from the surrounding counties as well. The ambush was to be an escalation of the rebellion which had recently been ignited by the Co. Tipperary ambush of Soloheadbeg, in which two Royal Irish Constabulary men were killed.

These attempts to disrupt the occupying force's communications lines, and indeed to uproot the 'invaders' entirely were taking place up and down the country for some time, but now new life had been breathed into the dream of independence.

The ambush they were planning, that cold December night, was the Pickardstown Ambush. It took place on the 7 January 1921, a good ninety years ago now. But you will still see people bless themselves as they pass Pickardstown Cross on the way between Tramore and Waterford City.

It was a time of oppression in every level in society. It was impossible to better yourself unless you fell in with the British occupiers and even then you had to watch every word you spoke and show deference to those who deemed themselves your superiors in every way.

You could not talk or walk freely in your own place. Imagine that! If you were out late, for any reason at all, even courting a girl, and were found walking or cycling home you could be thrown into the body of the jail or shot on the spot, for Military Law had been declared. Every move you made was monitored by the Royal Irish Constabulary (RIC) and they were living out among the people which made it easier for them.

Waterford City and county were particularly plagued because it was the first place the enemy would try to clear out and make his own. As a port city it had the disadvantage of being too accessible to invaders. They had a resident occupying army in the presence of the 1st Devonshire Regiment, whose HQ was in the military barracks in Barrack Street, inside in Waterford. There were more than a thousand troops there, including officers.

My late mother-in-law, Hannie Bolger, God be good to her now, used to live in Green Street, beside the barracks, when she was a girl. She used to tell the story of a man living in the houses there, once, who played the bugle. He was a soldier, but he got into trouble with a superior, inside the barracks and, by way of getting his own back, and venting his spleen on the whole company inside the walls, he got up in the middle of the night and sounded the reveille.

All the soldiers tumbled out of their bunks in great alarm and with much shouting of orders for they thought they were being attacked. He did it a few times and the soldiers went through all the houses in the area, as they say, like a dose of salts, searching for the culprit. She used to say that the British had no sense of humour for they shot the poor devil.

The town of Dungarvan was scalded by the presence of the East Kent Regiment and along the Waterford coast in the coastguard stations there were small detachments of the Royal Marines. They had the local RIC, who were the eyes and ears for the British and then the poor people were destroyed entirely, by the arrival of the worst of all; the Black & Tans.

I am sure you have heard of them. They were a bad lot and even when I was young my older sisters were afraid coming home from school in case there were Black & Tans hiding up in the fields above the road. This was many years after the Pickardstown Ambush.

The mention of the Black & Tans, even today will send a shiver of apprehension through most elderly people. Well, the decision to mount an ambush in Pickardstown, just outside the town of Tramore, was made by the gathering of men who had had enough, God help them.

There was a man called Paddy Paul and he was one of the local leaders, in those troubled times. He was a brigadier in the East Waterford Brigade. I know what you are thinking now. Who were this crowd? Well now, you didn't think that the men of Ireland were all lying down quiet under the yoke of the invader, did you? Not a bit of it, let me tell you, and the men of Co. Waterford can be a contrary lot, when someone tries to push them around in their own place. Small blame to them. They were what we now call the Old IRA and they had their own underground military with all the ranks and rules that any regular army would have, and, between you and me, they probably had a few more besides.

The biggest problem they had, however, was the lack of arms and ammunition, and the only way they could lay hands on these necessary items was to raid the RIC barracks or ambush soldiers on the roads. Raiding of RIC barracks had been carried out all over the county and some were even burnt down and abandoned entirely, as a result of attacks. So arms were being gained by the locals, little by little.

Now this ambush was to be carried out with the help of some of the West Waterford Brigade for they would not have been able to raise the number needed from East Waterford without attracting unwanted attention. The man in charge there was known as Pax Whelan. The day they planned to carry out the ambush, as I told you, was to be the 7 January 1921.

Their plan was daring but it seemed assured of success. They knew the ground they were working on and their own limitations with regard to arms and ammunition and experience. Surprise was to be the key to the success of this ambush.

You imagine them meeting that night, with lookouts posted nearby, tense and ready for action, the lowered voices, making the plans and issuing the instructions. Then the decision made and a sense of purpose pervading. There would have been an edge of fear there also, for even heroes know fear though they manage to overcome it. It would have been cold, but weather was not a consideration. The plan was to strike hard and fast and, most of all, to gain possession of more weapons and ammunition.

It was simple really. They needed to get some of the military out from the barracks in Waterford, not too many, but enough for them to get the better of. The only safe way to lure them out to where they planned the ambush was to have them called there by the local RIC who were stationed in their barracks in Queen Street, Tramore.

So it was planned that a small, but convincing, attack would be launched against the Police Barracks in Tramore. Their predicted response would be to seek help by sending up a Verey light or flare, which would be seen by the soldiers on duty at Waterford Military Barracks, 7 miles distant. This was the way they communicated the fact that they needed assistance and were being attacked. The military would then dispatch help and the trap would be sprung.

The site picked for the ambush was good. There was a railway bridge crossing over the Waterford to Tramore road known as the Metal Bridge. It was far enough outside Tramore to give them a fair chance of setting it up unseen and getting away afterwards, and at the last moment they would make a barricade across the road on the Tramore side of the bridge.

Close to this bridge, on the Waterford side, there was a convergence of three roads. One road came down from Ballinattin, another was the old Waterford Road and the last was the new main Waterford-Tramore Road. Up along the Ballinattin road and the old Waterford road there was higher ground which overlooked the main road on which they expected the soldiers from Waterford to come.

Further on, beyond the Metal Bridge and the proposed barricade, there was a small country road called the Glen Road, which cut off to the right of the main road. There was also the railway embankment overlooking the site. On the left-hand side of the road, the overgrown marshy area led down to the back strand of Tramore.

All of these positions made it possible for them to retreat back to their own areas, should anything go amiss.

Once these plans were laid in the late December, it was just a matter of letting everyone know where and when they must be ready. Also they would have included the local *Cumann na mBan* because these ladies were invaluable when it came to feeding, dressing wounds and hiding the men on the run. Once the ambush was over, some would definitely be in need of hiding. So the women made their preparations too and on the night of the ambush they had a supply of food ready for the men.

The volunteers from Waterford numbered around twenty and were led by a man called Willie Keane. Some of these proceeded to St Otteran's Mental Hospital where they had a secret arms dump in the grounds. Two of their volunteers worked in the hospital, so it was safe enough.

Armed now, they had to take every precaution not to be seen. It was easier then, because beyond the hospital grounds and Ballytruckle houses, there were fields mainly (although it is hard to imagine that today). They met up with the rest of their party at a safe farm near Kill St Laurence and the rifles, shot guns and ammunition were distributed. It was a local postman by the name of Tom Brennan who led them across country to Pickardstown cross.

They were the first to arrive and the night was bitter cold and starry bright.

In the meantime, from the other directions, volunteers had gathered and from Dunhill came around fourteen men, led by Jim Power. They came anyway they could, on bicycles and on foot. Armed with rifles and shotguns, they met in the dark of the evening at a farm near Carrickavantry, just above Tramore. They were supposed to wait there for the third group to come from Stradbally and Bunmahon.

A man had been dispatched earlier that day to meet with this group in Bonmahon, who were led by a man called Lennon and included one of the leaders of the plan, Pax Whelan.

Their strategy had been to commandeer three cars and to get there as quickly as possible, rather than secretly. But they were unfortunate in their choice of cars, for none of them were worth

a curse and kept breaking down. Remember that it was very early days in car manufacture and petrol would have been nearly impossible to obtain. Well, between the jigs and the reels, they took so long getting to the rendezvous that the Dunhill men decided to proceed to Pickardstown without them. Their nerves must have been on edge, waiting and wondering. They joined the Waterford men, who, by now, were very jumpy. It was almost eleven that night by the time the three groups were finally together. I bet there were some words spoken which could not be repeated here.

Now that they were all together, the time had come for action. It was probably welcomed by now. The attack on the police barracks was first and then, all going well, they would have a lorry, called a Crossley Tender, carrying twelve to fourteen soldiers, sent out from Waterford.

Brigadier Paddy Paul, himself, decided to lead this raid. He called for volunteers and the six men he chose to accompany him were Nicky Whittle, Jim Power, Martin Cullinane, Pat Keating, Pakeen Whelan and Mickie Bishop.

The thrill of excitement and the hot blood rising must have been great as they moved like shadows into the streets of Tramore. Now it is my belief that they had no intention of killing any of the resident RIC members who manned the Queen Street Police barracks. They just wanted to make it as realistic an attack as possible, so that help was called out from Waterford.

Inside in the barracks some ten constables and two sergeants relaxed in a false sense of security. Outside, under a starry sky, the volunteers crept into position. One went around the back of the building and the others took up various positions to the front.

In the way of many important fancy buildings of the time, the barracks had a lovely fanlight over the front door. Sure this was grand in ordinary times, but when you are under attack you might as well have no door. It was through this fanlight that one of the volunteers hurled one of the most deadly devices ever invented, the Mills bomb. When William Mills invented this devilish device, for the military, did it occur to him, I wonder, that his fellow countrymen would one day be on the receiving end of his invention?

Well the fanlight broke easily and once the bomb exploded, there was pandemonium. The sergeants shouted orders, constables scrambled for their weapons and a hail of rifle fire raked into the building from the front and rear. A constable went down, wounded in the thigh, and the decision was made. Send up a flare, get help. They had no way of knowing how many were outside and the shock of the grenade coming into their hallway triggered every instinct for self-preservation.

High into the night sky a flare from the Verey pistol soared and flared.

Outside, the attackers silently rejoiced and withdrew back into the shadowy ways and back down to Pickardstown cross. Once there, orders were given and the men took up their positions. They would not have long to wait. On to the higher ground of the Ballinattin road two groups were sent. They had rifles and shotguns. Michael McGrath and Thomas O'Brien were with them.

The junction of the old and new Waterford roads has a 'v'-shape receding up to higher ground and it was here, in the fields between, that four riflemen waited. On the railway embankment ten Dunhill men waited with shotguns. With the barricade now in place on the Tramore side of the Metal Bridge, the last group, from West Waterford, took up position, with rifles, on the Glen Road.

The starry night was bitter cold. Fingers were freezing. Hearts were thumping and every ear listening. The ground was cold and damp and the clothing they wore, despite many layers, gave little protection from the chill. Their breaths fogged the air.

Sound carries far at night and a sound came to them on the breeze. It was a minute or two before they were sure and then at a quarter to midnight the rumble of the approaching lorries came clear. There were quick indrawn breaths and whispers of 'Steady, now lads'.

As the sound drew nearer, headlights were suddenly spotted and they realised that the approaching lorries were not on the main road, as they had expected, but were coming down the old Tramore Road between the four riflemen and the groups on the Ballinattin Road. This was the first spanner in the works but could still be worked around, all it needed was patience. Let them get down onto the main road, under the railway bridge and to the barricade.

The rumble of the lorries increased and suddenly it came to the waiting men that there were more lorries than they expected, and a much larger force of arms to be dealt with. They could have very easily withdrawn then but just as the first of the lorries, filled to the gills with battle-ready soldiers, turned down on to the main road before the bridge, a shot rang out.

Who can say what happened. A frozen finger slipped maybe or a nervous young volunteer squeeze too hard on the trigger. Whatever the cause, everything changed once that shot rang out.

Two of the lorries were now on the old road and two were on the new road, and the now-alerted British soldiers had the advantage. The four lorries from Waterford held some forty to sixty soldiers and there were RIC members with them also. Worse still, three of them had come to a halt outside the ambush site.

It is easy to imagine the soldiers slipping quickly from the lorries to the shelter of the ditches. The volunteers opened fire again and they were quickly pinpointed by the British. There was a quick exchange of fire. The British realised that there were men on the Ballinattin Road and that they could, with stealth, come behind them.

Lt Frederick Charles Yoe was in command and he quickly gave the order that they should slip over the ditches and come behind the ambushers. He was a veteran of the First World War and well versed in military tactics. He directed them into the fields, behind the present-day shrine.

Caught between the British troops on the old road and also on the new road, the four riflemen, led by Tom Brennan, the postman, held still. As they lay there about twenty British soldiers passed within feet of them. They then began to withdraw and managed to cross the road further up in the hope of joining up with their comrades from the Ballinattin Road, whom they assumed would have begun to withdraw as well, seeing the superior forces. But the men on the Ballinattin Road were coming under heavy fire and finding it difficult to withdraw.

There would be no help from the other two groups on the railway embankment and the Glen Road, for they were short on ammunition and in danger of being cut off themselves. They withdrew any way they could and headed across country towards Dunhill, with the sound of gunfire ringing in the night air.

Withdrawing from their positions on the Ballinattin Road was nearly impossible because of the numbers of soldiers deployed against them. As some of the volunteers pulled back up the hill, Michael Wylie was shot in both legs and had to be carried to safety. When a volunteer by the name of O'Neill was trying to slip over a ditch with Michael McGrath he heard McGrath being captured behind him. McGrath had no chance at all, he was surrounded, and later they shot him in the head.

Scattered around the area there were still some of the volunteers trying to get away. A man by the name of Nicky Whittle, who was well known in the area, put up his head, during a lull in the gunfire, and promptly got shot twice. He took one bullet to his neck and the other to the small of his back. God help him, he couldn't do a thing, only lay there pretending to be dead as the soldiers came up to where he was.

He was shot a third time and he said himself after that he would have been done for except that a sound from the road further down caused the soldier, who was about to club him with the butt of his rifle, to pause and call out 'Halt, who goes there?' A voice answered 'Friend' and stepping out of the dark a man called Connie Dorgan, from Waterford, shot and wounded the soldier.

The British soldiers coming to their shot comrade's aid found the wounded Thomas O'Brien. He was out of ammunition and unable to get away. They vented their spleen on him, beating him with rifle butts and then, eventually, shot him. They left the three ambushers for dead and carried their wounded comrade back to the lorry on the road below.

But Nicky Whittle was not dead. He managed to crawl away into the dark of the night and with great difficulty made his way to a house which had a light on. God help the poor people, they must have got an awful fright when they saw him all covered in blood, but sure they couldn't let him stay there, so near to the action. They knew very well that all the houses in the area would be torn asunder in the searches which would follow the ambush.

He was helped to reach his cousin's house out near Ballygarron and they sent for a Dr Purcell, who could be trusted, to take care of him. In the days that followed he was transferred, with Michael Wyley, in secret, to St Otteran's Hospital. They would have been very much aware of all that was happening and the deaths of their comrades. It was a time of great danger for them and those who cared for them in the hospital. Word eventually came that the military were coming to search the hospital and the two were spirited away to safety. I never heard where Michael Wyley went but, can you imagine the irony of this, Nicky Whittle found refuge in England. The world is indeed a strange place.

The Pickardstown Ambush had failed badly and many of the volunteers were arrested and questioned brutally in the days that followed. The shooting of Michael McGrath and Thomas O'Brien further fuelled the determination of many to gain independence for Ireland.

I often heard people from Poleberry in Waterford, the place poor Michael McGrath came from, talk sadly about his passing, for he was well known and liked in his home place.

The thing which has scalded them most is the fact that his funeral became a focal point for more suppression by the British. He had been identified by his union card in a pocket and word had gone out and hundreds of mourners turned up at St John's Church, on 10 January. This probably worried the military and so the order was given that only forty mourners were allowed to attend.

It was only through the intervention of the then Mayor of Waterford City, Vincent White, that further bloodshed did not take place, such was the anger in the crowd. In the face of a heavily armed company of British soldiers he asked the people to return to their homes. The soldiers then went with the cortege to Crobally churchyard, where Michael McGrath was laid to rest beside his parents.

The British Army failed to identify the body of Thomas O'Brien and no one claimed him. Sure they couldn't, the *craturs*, without putting more people in danger. He was taken and buried at Ballygunner cemetery, on the Dunmore side of Waterford.

I have heard it said that on the day he was laid to rest he was prayed over by three priests and that the coffin was checked by the military to see if anyone had put a name on it. The records in Ballygunner Church have recorded his burial under 'anonymous', but sure everyone knows that Thomas O'Brien, who gave his life for Irish independence, lies there.

# 25

# THE
# SEAHORSE

*Did you ever hear the story of the wreck of the* Seahorse *in Tramore Bay? Well it is not a tale for the faint-hearted, for there was great loss of life under terrifying conditions.*

The *Seahorse* was a good name, according to old nautical traditions. It did not offend the sea spirits, as other names often did, so those who braved the might of the ocean, on board her, probably felt as safe as could be expected.

The shipwrights who made her used the best Irish oak and she started her life in London in 1784, which wasn't today or yesterday. She had three decks and three masts and was a grand vessel. She was made for the times that were in it, so for a time she was used as a frigate, which meant she was armed with canon and carried naval personnel. She was, according to some accounts, part of Lord Nelson's fleet at one time, but who knows, for down the years, there were many vessels named *Seahorse*.

When she was no longer required, or maybe no longer able for the hardship of fighting at sea, she was downgraded to become a 350-ton transport vessel. There was a different feel to a ship which was bringing troops and their families to and from destinations.

That is how it would have been, on board the *Seahorse*, the day she loaded up at Ramsgate, on the east coast of England. It is easy to imagine the bustle of loading, the shouts and calls, the smell of tar and fish and the tang of salt on the air. Perhaps too, there was still the smell of munitions on board, even transport vessels would keep small cannon on board, I'm sure.

They say that the *Seahorse* came into Ramsgate just before Christmas so that those aboard could spend Christmas at home. It appears she was carrying troops, and their followers, home from France, but they were already re-assigned to garrison duty in Cork. It is easy to think that they were only joined their by wives and children to go to, what would seem to them a safe enough duty, in Ireland.

The men, women and children of that time would have been dressed in a much different fashion than we have today. It was a time when gentlemen and officers would have worn fancy, lacy outfits, and wigs. The ordinary folk wore hats and long jackets and the women long skirts and shawls. The children would have worn long clothing also and pantaloons.

They would not have had suitcases to carry their belongings in either but would have had sea chests stowed away in the hold, carrying their few belongings.

They left the safe harbour of Ramsgate on 25 January 1816. The *Seahorse* was commanded by Capt. Gibbs, with an Irishman, John Sullivan, as first mate and a crew of seventeen. In port they had picked up a young Naval Officer, Lt Allen, who was on his way to join another vessel the *Tonnant*, in Cork. He probably felt more at home with the crew of the *Seahorse* than he did with her passengers. She was carrying the men of the 2nd Battalion 59th Regiment of Foot. There were sixteen officers, two-hundred-and-eighty-seven soldiers, thirty-three women and thirty-eight children. It was a very crowded vessel which sailed out on that cold but calm morning.

She was not alone as she embarked from Ramsgate, on that day, for travelling in sea convoy were two other ships also carrying troops to Cork. They were the brig *Boadicea*, also carrying the men of the 2nd Battalion 59th Regiment, who were returning from the Battle of Waterloo to garrison duty at Cork and the larger 818 ton *Lord Melville*, a former East India ship, carrying men of the 82nd Regiment.

Sailing ships were manoeuvred by using a wheel connected to the rudder, and sails. Usually the wheel would be manned by at least two sailors and they would have a type of sling slung around them so that if the ship hit rough weather they would not be swept away. It would have been noisy, with the creaking and groaning of timbers and the crack of canvas in the billowing sails. The rise and fall of the ship as she moved over the waves would have been difficult for some on board and more than likely many among them were sea sick; however, Cork was not a million miles away and they would be clear of the war ships further south so it would have been just a thing to get over.

They anchored overnight in a stretch of water known as the Downs. At daybreak she weighed anchor and continued on her journey. The weather had begun to pick up a little with light breezes blowing from the north/north-west. She sailed on and by midnight she was off Dungeness. By 28 January she was off Lizard's Point and the wind blowing from the south took her past the Wolf Rock, between Land's End and St Mary's on the Scilly Isles and out into St George's Channel. At this point everyone would have been on the alert, watching out for warships. The wind was increasing and below decks many would have begun to regret ever setting foot on board the gallant *Seahorse*.

If you have ever been at sea in rough weather you will know how difficult things can be, but this was now turning into a full-blown storm. It came from a south/south-easterly direction, pushing them hard onwards. In a short time, with the seas running high, they had lost sight of their companion ships of the convoy. They had no such thing as radio communication then. Any signalling between ships would have to have been in line of sight. With the raging seas and the increasing ferocity of the wind, the three ships were rising and falling out of sight very quickly. So in reality they were alone on the stormy seas.

Aboard the *Seahorse* they found it was impossible to get a proper bearing so the first mate, John Sullivan, who was the only man aboard who had any idea of the Irish coast, went up the rigging to see if he could get a bearing. Bless his brave heart, he struggled against terrible odds. It was all he could do to keep his grip as he climbed. The bitterly cold wind and rain lashed his eyes as he tried to catch a glimpse of land. His hands were frozen as he clung there. Then, disaster, he was ripped from the rigging with one fierce gust and came smashing down on the storm lashed forecastle. He was broken like a child's toy, his limbs and his insides, and there was no help for him, God save us, and he died, cradled in his wife's arms some three hours later.

It was the beginning of a terrible chain of events which those brave souls aboard the *Seahorse* endured. The Captain intended to head for the Kinsale Lights and sail down the coast to Cork but in the dark and the storm no fix of position was possible and it was with great relief they sighted Minehead in the early hours of the morning. They could also see Hook Lighthouse but the strength of the wind made it impossible for them to round Brownstown Head. Even in daylight there was no sign of their companion ships of the convoy.

They had no way of knowing that both the *Boadicea* and the *Lord Melville* were also in dire straights. The *Boadicea*, at this time, was being forced by the gale into the lee shore of Courtmacsharry Bay and went on the Curlane Rocks that same day. Most of the crew and passengers, numbering 255, were drowned.

The *Lord Melville* struck the rocks 300 yards off the Old Head of Kinsale and a boat was sent out to help them but it and its crew of twelve men were drowned. Those aboard the *Lord Melville* would eventually be rescued by the men of Kinsale Head Lighthouse.

The *Seahorse* had taken a terrible beating. Her mainsail was ripped to ribbons and her foremast had gone over the side into the raging sea. Her anchors dragged and she was drifting into Tramore Bay where she grounded less than a mile from shore, just in near Brownstown Head. They say that the decks were lined with soldiers and terrified passengers, God help them, they had no hope for the lifeboats were already torn away. It was here she began to

break up. Many jumped and tried to swim to safety but many were more afraid of the rage of the sea and were already injured and terrified beyond reason.

The people on the shore had watched her terrible dilemma but were unable to do anything to save her. Men climbed out on rocks and tried to help those who managed to swim ashore. There are stories of how some clung to the broken timbers of the ship and managed to reach safety. One account tells of a man who was impaled on the nails in the planks but they held him safely until he drifted ashore. In all, only thirty souls survived out of all those lovely people who left Ramsgate, aboard the *Seahorse*, just five days before.

In the days and weeks that followed this terrible tragedy bodies were washed ashore along with other wreckage. A mass grave was first made down near the sand hills for all the deceased while the locals took care of the survivors as best they could.

In later years it was decided to remove their remains to a safer higher ground. An obelisk marks a burial plot at the Church of Ireland, on Church Road. If you go out along the Doneraile Walk you will come across a large monument commemorating the passing of so many souls in the wreck of the *Seahorse*. It overlooks the scene of the tragedy. Where the sea eddies in and out between the rocks below, it is easy to imagine, as was reported, that in the days that followed the tragedy, the flotsam and jetsam washed into the little coves included the sodden wigs of the gentlemen and officers.

The destruction of the *Seahorse* and the loss of so many lives caused the Admiralty to take notice of Tramore Bay. Lloyds of London funded the building of piers, including the erection of the Metal Man on Newtown Head to prevent further calamities. Some five years later, in 1821, those responsible for looking after the Port of Dublin decided that they would erect three towers on Great Newtown Head and two on Brownstown Head, where the *Seahorse* had struggled in its last hours.

It was another two years before the five pillars, which are still standing there today, were built. On the centre pillar at Newtown Head they placed a huge figure of a Metal Man who has his hand extended in warning – Keep out good ship, keep out from me, for I am the rock of misery.

The Metal Man figure is about 14 feet tall with each pillar approximately 61 feet high. A romantic legend says that if a girl succeeds in hopping around the Metal Man pillar three times on one foot she will be married within the year.

# 26

# THE
# CROPPY BOY

*There was an adult story told when we were young, and we were hunted off to bed if it came up in discussion, and it often did, for to the old people the rebellion of 1798 was as close as yesterday, in their minds. I remember Denny Maher, God rest his gentle soul, saying that the people who carried out atrocities, which included the use of the pitch cap and the rack and much worse, were not fit to be called humans. The word then would be, 'Shush now don't be giving the children nightmares'. Well, they are all dead and gone now, bless them, so I will tell this story as gently as it is possible.*

As you know well, Ireland has been troubled by invaders. Wouldn't you think, now, that they would have enough to do looking after their own places, instead of coming over here and destroying and taking over things? Not a bit of it, this little island of ours is like honey to a bee. Since the Danes first landed, they all think they must have a share of it. Well by the time the years had gone by up to 1798, there were more English soldiers and landlords over here than there were our own people. They were pushing and shoving the Irish off the good land and taking it over themselves, and it was no wonder at all, then, that the Irish rose up once again in great anger.

In the history books it is called the Rebellion of 1798, and it is a cold and heartless title to a time when terrible things were done, on both sides mind you, breaking the minds and hearts of poor people.

Well, in a place called Passage East, in Co. Waterford, they were too handy to the reach of the English and the rebels there suffered cruelly. There was an army barracks just up the road a bit, out of Passage village. It was called Geneva Barracks and it was built on a site that had been allocated to a group of merchants and tradesmen from Geneva, in Switzerland, to set up a trading place of their own. However, there were too many disputes between the people from New Geneva, as they called it, and the authorities, so the trading place never happened. Then when the French Revolution started, the English got very jumpy and took over that area to make it into a barracks.

Geneva Barracks was big enough to hold around 2,000 soldiers and they had a high wall built all around the acres and acres of it. Some say it was more than 12 acres but who is to know truly for all that is left to us now is some ruins. It is said also that in more recent times a man who lived in Dungarvan got ownership of the buildings from Lord Beresford, and he had lots of the stonework taken away down to Dungarvan for use in a place he owned there. That man was called Galway. The first military there were known as the Tyrone Militia. It soon turned into a prison of ill repute for the Irish rebels.

The soldiers were cruel and heartless and made the lives of the ordinary people in the area very uncomfortable indeed. No one knew when they were going to be turned out of their beds and hauled off on the charge of being a 'croppy', or of giving sustenance to a croppy. The fashion at that time was for most men to have long hair, and the wearing of wigs by the officers and gentlemen was normal. In France the revolutionaries cut their hair short and many in Ireland copied them. Having short or cropped hair gave them the name croppies.

Well to get back to our own Croppy Boy, he was a young man caught up in the rebellion and was doing what he felt was right and just for his own country. At that time, there were strong feelings among the deeply religious young men that they should go to confession before they went to fight. They wanted to make their peace with God just in case they were killed in action. Now, not all of the priests then were sympathetic to the cause, but there were some and these would have been known to the rebels. Indeed some priests were subjected to all sorts of persecution themselves, and they had seen the terrible cruelties inflicted on the people in their spiritual care.

The croppy boy, who remains nameless, went to the church in the dark of the evening to confession and to be blessed. He asked for the local priest, who was known as Fr Green, and was told to go on inside as the priest was already in there and would hear his confession. He entered into the dimly-lit church (sure, they had no electric light then) and saw a priest seated on a chair, which was normal, and he went and knelt beside him and began his confession. The priest said nothing, and as he finished he waited for

the blessing, but instead of a blessing, the man he had taken for a priest leapt up in rage and threw off the priest's robe. It was a Yeoman captain from Geneva Barracks. Sure, what chance did the lad have? He was surrounded in no time at all and taken off to the Barracks where he was duly executed.

He was one of many to be executed there, some after terrible torture and harm. It is said that if a woman was taken by the soldiers, on any suspicion at all, she would be subjected to what they called 'blanketing', which meant she would be tossed up and down on a sheet or blanket in her naked state until she was almost dead or died from her injuries.

You know, even though we heard about these things when we were young we didn't fully understand that the stories reflected the true history. We thought that they were just stories embellished by our elders. It was a terrible, frightening thing to come to the realisation that not only were these stories about the croppies true, but that the treatments meted out to them was kept on record by their captors.

The memory of the Croppy Boy is kept alive through a memorial stone. In the chancel of the ruined medieval church at Crooke, just above the village of Passage East, is a whitewashed marker which is said to mark the grave of the Croppy Boy, the 'Unknown Soldier' of the 1798 Rebellion.

As with many of our best stories it is very much alive in song. To this day you can hear the ballad of 'The Croppy Boy', sung with great empathy, when people gather together, for any celebration, in the south-east region.

There is a further memorial to this unknown Croppy Boy in the form of a famous painting by British/Canadian artist Charlotte Schreiber. The painting, titled 'The Croppy Boy (The Confession of an Irish Patriot)', is held in the National Gallery of Canada.

I do not know a better way to finish this story than to include the song itself. This song was first published in *The Nation* newspaper. It was written by James McBurney from Co. Down. It is sung to a traditional air known as '*Cailín Ó Cois tSúire Mé*' – 'I am the girl from beside the River Suir':

'Good men and true in this house who dwell,
To a stranger bouchal I pray you tell:
Is the priest at home, or may he be seen?
I would speak a word with Father Green.'

'The Priest's at home, boy, and may be seen;
'Tis easy speaking with Father Green.
But you must wait till I go and see
If the holy Father alone may be.'

The youth has entered an empty hall;
What a lonely sound has his light footfall
And the gloomy chamber's chill and bare,
With a vested Priest in a lonely chair.

The youth has knelt to tell his sins:
'*Nomine Dei*,' the youth begins
At '*mea culpa*' he beats his breast,
And in broken murmers he speaks the rest.

'At the siege of Ross did my father fall,
And at Gorey my loving brothers all.
I alone am left of my name and race;
I will go to Wexford and take their place.

'I cursed three times since last Easter day;
At mass time once I went to play;
I passed the churchyard one day in haste,
And forgot to pray for my mother's rest.

'I bear no hate against living thing,
But I love my country above my king.
Now, Father, bless me and let me go
To die, if God has ordained it so.'

The priest said nought, but a rustling noise
Made the youth look up in wild surprise;
The robes were off, and in scarlet there
Sat a yeoman captain with fiery glare.

With fiery glare and with fury hoarse,
Instead of blessing, he breathed a curse:
'Twas a good thought, boy, to come here to shrive,
For one short hour is your time to live.

Upon yon river three tenders float;
The priest is in one – if he isn't shot
We hold his house for our Lord the King,
And, amen say I, may all traitors swing.'

At Geneva Barrack that young man died,
And at Passage they have his body laid.
Good people who live in peace and joy,
Breathe a prayer, shed a tear for the Croppy Boy.

There are other versions of this story which are well known. The version which is sung on the Wexford side of the river has a verse which states:

As I was walking up Wexford Street,
My own true father I chanced to meet
My own true father did me deny
And the name he called me was the Croppy Boy.

This could have been about a different Croppy Boy, for there were many, but the air of the tune is the same. In the Waterford version he claims 'At the siege of Ross did my father fall.'

There is a further leg to this story – the British Soldiers had a song known as 'Croppies Lie Down' in which the soldiers are the heroic ones. Isn't every story dependent on a person's point of view?

# 27

# LACKENDARA
# JIM

My parents often mentioned the 1914/18 war or the Great
War. They would talk about it as though it had only happened.
My father was born in 1901 and so would have been just reaching
his teen years when the whole world was at war. They would talk
about people who had 'gone away' to war and never returned or
who returned so broken and changed that they had no real life left
to them when they came home. The talk would ebb and flow as to
the rights and wrongs of the fighting itself and then to the treatment of the poor men who came home.

These men had championed the downtrodden, like knights of old,
but were cast aside by ignorant people who knew little or nothing
about the real horrors of fighting their fellow men. My mother, God
rest her, used to say that the politicians who sent men to fight should
themselves lead, not be sitting comfortably on their soft backsides.
Then she would blush and my father would clear his throat, which
we knew was to hide a laugh, and she would add defiantly that if
women were running the world it would be a much better place.

When we were children it was common to see old men with one
leg gone, or who had lost an eye or, bless us and save us all, seemed
a little bit soft in the head. Some of these poor men were from the
Second World War but some were too old for that to have been

the case. I have a memory of a very old man who used to sleep in a little lean-to shed outside the house where I was born and no one talked about where he came from or how. He would never come in the house, even on the coldest of nights and nothing my mother or father could say would persuade him. They used to bring out the tea and food to him. He helped around the land and gardens. We understood that he couldn't feel comfortable in a house anymore and needed peace and quiet.

Well, so it was too with Lackendara Jim, the Hermit of the Comeragh Mountains. Some people, talking about him now would refer to him as 'The Rockman' but mainly they name him Lackendara.

He was born in Castlereagh, near the mountain known as Lackendara in the Comeragh range in Co. Waterford. His given name was James Fitzgerald and the year of his birth was 1883. He was a country lad, brought up away from the turmoil of city life.

His early days would have been alive with the stories of what was happening around the country. These stories would have come by word of mouth mainly. It was a time of fear and despair for many poor people. Evictions were happening all over Ireland and there was a wickedness abroad among landlords and in particular absentee landlords. They distanced themselves from the plight of their tenants and thought nothing of sending in heavy-handed military or police to clear out their tenants from the hovels they were occupying on the land.

He would have known all about rack rents, where the landlords put up the rents so high that no tenant could afford them and so could be turned out. Bless us and save us, they even tried to tax the God-given light by taxing extra if you had a window in your little one-roomed home.

Times were desperately hard for the ordinary people who lived on the land, and people were starting to fight back. They had no other option. Members of the Irish Land League were actively engaged in the Land War and Parnell and Davitt were imprisoned in Kilmainham.

Lackendara Jim would have known about the politicians seeking Home Rule and he would certainly have heard of John Redmond who was very active in Co. Waterford. It was John Redmond, leader of the Irish Party, who encouraged the young men to join the British Army, saying that by showing loyalty in this Great War, their sacrifices would be rewarded by Westminster, who would have to agree to their political demands, when they came back.

He dangled the lure of a steady wage and a separation allowance for married men, if they joined the British Army. To young men of Lackendara's age, he was eighteen when the Great War began, it was no contest. There was nothing to keep him in Ireland; no prospects, and fear and depression all around. So in 1914 Lackendara Jim left the comfort of his grandparent's home and joined the British in their fight against the Ottoman forces. He was not alone in what he did for, according to the records, more than 200,000 Irish people served in the allied forces in the Great War.

If the poor devil had known that he was in reality only protecting the Anglo Persia Oil Company and their claim on the oil wells, which they had taken over, he might have thought twice about putting his own life on the line.

Lackendara Jim did not have his well-known name when he joined up so he was more than lightly called Fitz or Fitzy by his companions in arms. Who knows? The training he went through would have been minimal and probably brutal in itself because the war was swallowing up the lives of those already in the field, and there would have been a rush on to get new recruits out and battle-ready.

Maybe, on the very ship which took Jim Fitzgerald away from Waterford, there were the famous cargos of donkeys which left the docks in Waterford to act as pack animals in the war. He might have left from Cork as it all depended on where he signed up. Life was so different then that it is hard for us to imagine. He soon found himself in a place with a biblical name, Mesopotamia, but there was nothing holy about the conditions that war-torn place presented to him and the many thousands of soldiers who, according to military records, fought some of the bloodiest battles ever. The name of that place today is Iraq.

He would have seen the great rivers, the Euphrates and the Tigris. His food rations would have been poor and his clothing inadequate for the terrain. His companions would have suffered from all sorts of illness such as cholera, which killed many, including their officers. He would have known about the siege of Kut-al-Amara and its surrender to the Ottoman forces. Perhaps he was with the British forces that stole across the River Tigris and bypassed the Ottoman forces to take back that place called Kut.

If only we had known the right questions to ask our own Lackendara. On the other hand he might not have wanted to answer such detailed questioning. The losses in that campaign came to a terrifying 92,000 British souls. Wasn't it a wonder to the world that he came home safe to the Comeragh Mountains?

It was 1918 when he came back home and found that the world had moved on in Ireland as well. Lord love him, his grandparents, who had reared him, Brigid and Martin, were gone to their eternal reward and there was little welcome for the soldiers of the British Army. Forgotten was the fact that there was no work or prospects when he left, four years previously.

Ireland had become a bitter and resentful nation as a result of the executions which followed the 1916 Easter Rising. Lackendara Jim had been up to his eyes in desert sand and muddy waddies fighting the Turk, protecting the new-found oil wells owned by the Anglo Persian Oil Co. when the shots rang out and James Connolly slumped dead in his seated position in Kilmainham. It was all news to him when he came home. Unwelcome news indeed, as he was war-weary already and his poor head still rang with the sound of exploding shells and constant gunfire.

Ireland was aflame with rebellion and many returned soldiers now found themselves hunted and despised. Some, however, formed the Cork Rangers and these, with their military training, were invaluable in the times to follow in Ireland.

Jim Fitzgerald had no heart any more for fighting. He had seen such cruelties and atrocities that his very soul was sore. There was no choice for him. He had to be away from people. The hurt and damage his heart and soul had suffered made him unable to settle into a house, be it ever so grand. He made his way up into the Comeraghs, sure he knew them well, from what must have seemed

a long time ago. He settled in a place near Coumshingaun Lake, called Kilclooney. The shelter he made there would have been better than many a place he had rested in during his soldiering time. Most of all it was quiet and there were no people.

The place he made for sleeping he lined with sheep's wool, which was plentiful on the mountains. He gathered rocks and built a make-shift kitchen which he roofed with tar barrel tops. These were easy enough to carry up to where he needed them. He blocked off gaps in the rocky walls with mud and grass and found a sort of peace in his solitude.

He didn't entirely live wild off the land and had his army pension to call on for food and other essentials. He would come down to collect the pension and was well known in a pub called Flynn's in Clonea. The people who knew him and his story were good to him and if there were explosions or thunderstorms they would always check on him for the noise would drive his poor head crazy and he would be 'out of his wits' with it.

The name he was now called was Lackendara Jim and that was to stay with him for the rest of his days. He wandered the mountains and spent the rest of his life there. The weather did not drive him down, either heat or freezing cold. The years rolled by, Ireland became independent, industry and culture again became possible but Jim stayed where he was.

He went up into the Comeraghs when he returned from the Great War in 1918 and lived his life as he chose until the year 1959, when he passed away three days after his 76th birthday.

There is a record of one time when he was interviewed by *Wide World Magazine* in 1954, where he is quoted as saying, 'I want to be at peace with the world and where can one find greater peace than in this elevated land from which I can see five counties on a fine day.' There are also some photographs in existence from times when he was content to pose with some locals who had cameras. These you can find for yourself on that great modern communication vehicle – the internet.

# 28

# THE WELLINGTON BOMBER AT THE SIXCROSSROADS

*I was in a house once and an elderly gentleman showed me a piece of metal, which he swore came from a crashed aeroplane during the war. Thinking it was when he was abroad and he young, I asked where the plane crashed and I remember laughing when he said it was out the Co. Waterford at the Sixcrossroads. I was thinking, at the time, of my brother-in-law, Joe Wall, who used to display cuts and grazes to his children and explain how he was injured in the war or by Red Indians. 'Another Waterford tall tale', I said.*

*Sure ignorance is bliss and what did I know? The man was right. It happened in February 1943 and he said that once, the locals got over the initial fright and discovered that no one was killed, then they commenced to pick up 'souvenirs' – until they were chased off by the Gardaí and the LDF (Local Defence Force).*

It was a bright moonlit night when the Wellington Bomber, returning from a raid on the U-boats in the port of Lorient, temporarily lost their navigator through unconsciousness from lack of oxygen. When he came to they were well and truly off course. They came in low over the south-east coast of Ireland and were seen by the many Coastwatchers and the Gardaí in Tramore and in as far as Kilmacow. The men on duty at the Military Barracks in Waterford kept a watchful eye on its circling course.

The crew of the Wellington had no idea that they were over neutral Ireland, except that some lights were showing, which would not have been the case over the English coast where a full blackout was in place. They came in so low that they could see the houses and followed the line of Waterford Harbour before circling for a while in a vain attempt to identify a landmark of some sort.

Hearing the heavy drone of the aircraft and knowing full well that London had, in recent weeks been bombed, the people of Waterford ran out into the streets. They could see the bomber clearly in the moonlight and those who where more knowledgeable about markings on planes, soon pronounced that it was not the Germans but a Wellington Bomber gone astray.

It was a great relief that they were not going to be bombed but they were now worried that the plane would crash on top of the houses, as it was circling so low. No one was going back to bed now, and held in the grip of fear and excitement, they watched as it circled and slowed.

I was told, by Dick Power, that the plane was so low and the air vibrating so much that at the top of the town, in an old house, which was riddled with damp, the wallpaper actually slid slowly down the wall, as it passed over.

On board the cruising aircraft the pilot, Sgt John Holloway, Sgt David Ross, the navigator, and Sgt George Slater, the radio operator came to the decision that with the fuel so low now, the only strategy open to them was to land somewhere. They had failed to make any contact with their own base, which was far away at Croft Airfield in Yorkshire.

They spotted a suitable field just beyond Waterford City and prepared for a crash landing. On the ground the people were already moving. They could see clearly that it was coming down in the fields beyond Kilbarry. With a decreasing roar, it glided in over Galvin's house near the Sixcrossroads and ploughed across the field, coming to rest halfway through the fence into the next field.

You can imagine what was in the minds of the people as they ran towards the site of the crash. The Galvin family came out of

their home like scalded cats, as the roof slates rattled, thinking they were being bombed. It must have been a great relief to them to see the path made by the bomber, gouged out through Dalton's field. Next thing must have been the fear that it would explode and still manage to kill them all.

A short way into the field, they saw one of the airmen gather himself and limp along the track to the plane, carrying his boot in his hand. This was Sgt Thomas, who had been thrown out of his rear gunner position by the first impact.

They were further startled then by a loud explosion from the aircraft and the flames leaped high into the sky, lighting the way for those hurrying out from the town.

When the Wellington finally came to a stop, the pilot, Sgt John Holloway, had sustained a head injury but was mobile. Sgt Slater took command and activated the delayed-action explosive device, which every war plane carried, to destroy secret equipment or documents held on board. The crew had then dashed for cover and waited, still unaware that they were in neutral Ireland.

The crowds hurrying to the scene were in high excitement, as they converged on the field. Dick Power related how he was taken out to the scene on the bar of his father's bicycle. Sgt Slater, the radio operator, now in command, went to meet the people coming across the field. Lord only knows, what was on his mind as he went slowly towards the advancing crowd. He probably noted, with relief, that they were not shooting at him and once he spoke to the first he met, he called out to the rest of the crew that they were in a friendly country.

The crew were taken to Galvin's house and the pilot's head injury cared for and they were fed by Mrs Galvin.

Across the field the bomber still blazed merrily away and, despite the danger from exploding ammunition from the machine guns on board, young boys and men crowded towards the downed aircraft. Bits and pieces were scattered in a trail across the field where the undercarriage had come away.

The Gardaí arrived on the scene shortly after, followed by the Local Defence Force from the Military Barracks. They did their best to keep people back from danger. The British airmen were taken into Waterford Military Barracks where they were held until they were shifted to the internment camp in the Curragh, in Kildare.

Well, need I tell you, there were many boys missing from school in the days that followed this event. Even though the Gardaí and Military had been stationed around the crash site, it was possible to get close to have a look and pick up the odd souvenir. According to reports, when Comdt Mackay, the Military Intelligence Officer, came to view the site he was stunned to be met by hundreds of men, women and children, with scraps of the plane, as souvenirs, going towards Waterford.

He had some words to say about that, to those on duty at the scene. After that it was much more difficult for the lads to gain access and in a few days a salvage crew arrived from Baldonnel

Aerodrome and removed all the wreckage. Sure they didn't take home the half of it, the boys and men of Waterford had bits on display for years after. Sure, didn't I see it myself?

Many aircraft, both British and German, came down in the south-east corner of Ireland. Some with disastrous results and in one case, as in Crobally, Tramore, a British aircraft landed intact and was subsequently acquired by the Irish Government for the Irish Army Air Corps.

With the passing of years, old documents have become available with regard to lots of military activity during the Second World War.

We can still find people, in Waterford City and County, who remember this period of our history very clearly.

My thanks to Richard Power, Rtd Comdt, 'D' Coy 9th Infantry Battalion FCA, Waterford, for his memories.

*For anyone interested in historical facts and figures, a man called Patrick J. Cummins has compiled a great historical record called* 'Emergency': Air Incidents South-East Ireland 1940-1945.

# 29

# THE REPUBLICAN PIG AND THE SIEGE OF WATERFORD

*The City of Waterford has been under siege many times and while the most famous was when Strongbow took the city, a much more recent siege, in 1922, still fires the imagination. As the saying goes, it is a siege that happened 'in living memory'.*

*Almost every second family, living in Waterford, has a story about this siege but my personal favourite is this one.*

It was during the 'Troubles'. We are the only nation in the world with the sense of humour to call our civil war dismissively 'the time of the Troubles.' Maybe we couldn't face the fact that brother was fighting against brother in a bloody war. By classing it as just 'Troubles' made it more 'family' and our own bit of bother. Sure it covered a multitude of violent acts that most families would rather not recall.

Anyway, to get back to my story, there were two sides engaged in the 'Troubles'. The Freestaters and The Republicans. One side were for the partitioning of Ireland and the others said it should be all or nothing.

Caught up in this, bickering and fighting, was Ernest Evans, a Welsh butcher, who had married an Irish girl from the banks of the River Suir. He never pretended to understand the 'Troubles' and had one aim, and that was to keep out of it and to take care of his family and his 'own business'. Everyone had to eat, whether they were Freestaters or Republicans, he reasoned. So he butchered animals of every sort for both factions.

He carried on his butchery business from the cool blue and white tiled ground floor of Kilaspy House. The spacious, arched work area included long marble slabs, pickling vats, salting tables, a great black range which was always in use, cooking hams for the shops, inside in Waterford.

It opened out into an enclosed courtyard where ponies and horses were stabled, on the far side, and dove-coots overhead were filled with the gentle cooing of a great many birds. A penny-far-thing bike lay permanently at the ready in case a boy might need to take an urgent message into Waterford City or to the surrounding countryside. There was a horse-drawn 'spring car', for important business, and a pony's trap at the ready also.

People called by to make arrangements to bring a beast for slaughter and Pat Ryan was one such man. The only difference being that Pat Ryan never managed to get his pig slaughtered. He was fond of the pig, you see, and even named him, like you would a Christian. Pigwig he called him. Well, the pig accompanied Pat Ryan wherever he went and they were both known far and wide. Sometimes it seemed that Pat was in charge but more often than not it looked like Pigwig was leading him a merry dance.

People had sympathy for Pat and he tormented with a wander-ing pig. This notion amused Pat but he played on it. Why wouldn't he? A man with a wandering pig could go places, and be seen in areas that no one else would get away with. As Pat said himself, a man on his own was suspicious, given the times that were in it, but a man chasing a pig, got sympathetic looks and often got help from the very people he was watching.

You see Pat Ryan was not an innocent man cursed with a wandering pig, at all. Nor could you call him a spy for, in all honesty, it began by him noticing things and realising early on that the pig, he was taking to be slaughtered, was as good a cover for his covert undertakings, as any he could have dreamed up. Pat Ryan became the eyes and ears for the Republican side in the 'Troubles' and Pigwig was his *aide de camp*.

Together they wandered in and out of towns and villages. The cheeky devil once even managed to chase the pig into the military barracks in Waterford. The sentries on duty were taken by surprise as the pig darted between them and Pat followed him, shouting and cursing his misfortune to own such an unruly pig.

After that foray, Pat reported back, triumphantly, that the Devonshire Regiment were in the process of pulling out. This cheered the Republican side no end. If they timed things right they could occupy the barracks within days of the departure of the British soldiers.

The night before Pigwig was, once again, scheduled to be slaughtered saw Pat and Pigwig journeying down the River Suir, under cover of dark, to a rendezvous not far from Waterford City. Pat tried his best to be quiet as he rowed but it is not easy, in the silence of the night, to quiet a pig and lessen the creaking of the oars at the same time.

They pulled into the bank at the appointed place and it was a miracle that neither of them got shot, for the sentry on lookout duty was jumpy and tired. At Pat's whispered word, that he would not be on duty there the following night, the man cheered up. He would see real action, at last, if Pat was right, and he generally was.

'General Prout is on the march and they are almost as far as Kilmacow and the bloody locals are feeding them', continued Pat. The sentry spat in disgust. 'I can't understand it at all', he said softly. 'How can men like the O'Briens and Sean Walsh, who fought beside us up until a few weeks ago, now be so dead against us?'

'I was discussing that very same thing with Pigwig here, and we coming down the river', said Pat. 'The conclusion we came to was that it is all down to pride, men's stupid pride.'

'I am not sure I understand you', said the sentry.

'Well this is how it was. Our lads went over to England and talked with Chamberlain and Lloyd George, oh two slippery rogues, if you ask me. Sure they talked rings round our lads and they did not understand fully what was being proposed, but were too proud to say so.'

'I don't know but you are right, but you better get yourself inside now, they are all waiting for your news.'

Well, on the morning that Pat Ryan and Pigwig were to come, once again, to have Pigwig slaughtered, things were stirring early in the Evans household. Ernest's wife, whom he always addressed as 'Missis' was busy collecting the eggs, from the many hens they owned, and she was being helped by their only son, Davy.

Davy was coming up on twelve years of age and had a deep fascination with his father's business. He loved the blood and the gore, once the terrible deed was done. He didn't much care for the actual killing although he pretended he did, to see his mother's reaction. He had been promised again and again that he could place the bucket for catching the blood on the day that Pigwig would be killed. Sure hadn't Pat Ryan, himself, promised him so, along with the promise of a new tin whistle from 'Hen' Sutton's shop, in Ferrybank.

Davy was beside himself with excitement. Today was sure to be the day but Ma seemed to have other ideas. He had heard her telling his Da that Pat Ryan would come in his own time and that was never when he was expected. She was insisting that Da and Davy go with her into the town to do the shopping, and help her carrying the bowls of dripping and the fresh eggs, for which she had taken orders.

If Da came with them they could bring the pony and trap so they would be back quicker, thought Davy, and besides, if Da was with himself and Ma in town, then Pigwig wouldn't be killed until they were all home. But Da was not falling in with the plan at all. He could hear them from the kitchen. Da was writing out the dockets for the sale of the eggs and dripping and he said loudly that he could not go to town this day. Da spoke kind of funny, him being Welsh, you see. He wanted Ma to go to the bank as well, to send a bank draft to the old people back home in Tonapandy. That was a change, thought Davy, for Da always liked to do his 'own business' as he put it.

Well, here they were now gathering the last of the eggs and hoping to make another full dozen. The broody hen insisted on sitting on as many eggs as she could and it was Davy's task to get them from under her. She had a beak like a razor and in desperation Davy threatened to wring her neck if she didn't stop pecking at him. His scandalised mother shouted at him to lift the silly hen off and hurry with the eggs or they would never reach town. Davy muttered vengeance on the world if he missed placing the bucket for Pigwig's blood.

It took another twenty minutes before they set off down the long winding avenue which would take them out onto Ballyrobin Road and thence to Ferrybank, across the Bridge of Waterford and in to Wall's shop in Arundel Square. Da had warned and warned Ma that she should not talk politics with anyone and she had been sharp with him. The best part of that had been when Ma said that all Da thought of was meat and money and that she could trip and fall, carrying all the messages. Da had looked at her in a funny, soft way, and told her she was a fine shapely woman with two great legs under her and she would never fall, especially if she went in and had some tea and sweet cakes when she reached town.

Ma had smiled then and straightened her blue hat, with the peacock's feather on it, and nodding she picked up the baskets and loaded Davy with some more and they set out.

Davy never minded the journey with Ma. They walked it often together. Sometimes she sang as they went and other times they talked and made plans. This day she was thinking about how much money they would get for the eggs and dripping as she wanted to buy some calico. Davy was thinking about the tea and cakes and hurrying back to catch Pigwig's blood. Da said it would make great black puddings.

The cobble stones of the streets in Waterford were hurting Ma's feet through her buttoned-up leather boots. She was dying for tea, and for that Davy was grateful. They went towards the usual eating house. It was O'Brien's, in Patrick Street. The streets seemed busier than usual and people were hurrying. As they rounded the corner onto Patrick Street, Davy stopped in his tracks. Ma bumped into him.

'Look Ma, look that man has a Tommy gun and he is kissing a girl'

'Oh the Lord save us', said his mother in a scandalised tone of voice. 'The hussy, and the whole of Patrick Street looking at her.'

'Is it a real gun Ma?' Davy tugged urgently at her sleeve.

'Never mind the gun now Davy, get in there and we will get a cup of tea.'

They pushed open the door and stepped into the warm interior, where the smell of fresh-baked bread and cakes was almost too much for Davy to bear, except that he kept looking back out the street window at the man with the gun.

He heard his mother ordering tea and cakes, and then horror of horrors the girl behind the counter said that they were closing and she couldn't serve them. Ma was raging and gave out to the girl. The girl said she was sorry but everyone was closing up shop and that they ought to get back across the bridge before it went up, in any case.

Ma said they would wait until the bridge went down, after the boat passed, but the girl was nearly doing a jig now.

'You don't understand Mrs. Evans' she said 'It won't be going down. That's our Marie out there, she's in the *Cumann na mBan* so she told us, and they are saying goodbye just in case.'

'Won't be going down, what do you mean, young woman?'

'Mrs Evans there is going to be a siege; you need to go home now. They are putting up the bridge.'

'A siege? Oh the Lord save us all. Come on Davy quick now.'
Davy heard the fear in Ma's voice but he didn't understand the cause.

'What's a siege Ma? Can we go home now and see Pigwig getting killed?'

The girl handed Ma a bag with some cakes in it, 'For the child', she said, and Ma fumbled for the money but the girl ushered them out of the shop saying they would be stale if she didn't take them, anyway.

Davy saw more men with different types of guns as they hurried along O'Connell Street, heading for the bridge. Ma was out of breath when they broke out on to the Quays, but Davy was leppin' with excitement. People were pushing and shoving and women with prams hurrying children. There were lots of men with guns at the bridge and some of them were shouting loudly at the people to move on quickly.

Just as they came across the road to the bridge a shot rang out and people screamed, and ducked down. Women and children ran on across the bridge but Ma and Davy were too late. A big sergeant blocked the way and would not let them pass. Davy could see the bridge starting to open up beyond the sergeant. There were men turning great big wheels to draw it up and it was groaning and clanking. Davy thought it was great fun. Then another shot rang out and the men with the guns pushed everyone back down and orders were given for the men around them to start shooting at the snipers on Mount Misery.

Ma was nearly fainting. She kept saying, 'But Mister, we have to get across, we have to get home to my husband. He is Welsh, you see, and he doesn't understand about these politics and shootings. He will be worried sick. We have to go.'

The man said, firmly, 'Sorry Mam, I cannot risk my men going out there to let down the bridge, not even for the Pope himself. You will have to find lodgings somewhere, and I need you to get back out of the way now.'

Back in Kilaspy, Ernest Evans was deep in conversation with Pat Ryan. He had just come in the courtyard with Pigwig. 'Where's Davy? I have his tin whistle for him?'

Ernest smiled as he eyed Pigwig up and down the long plump length of him. 'There is nothing to beat the White York, is there?' he said admiringly. 'The lad and the Missis are gone to town, this day, and lucky I am that I was not made to go with them. I was glad you were coming Mr Ryan, or she would have walked the legs off me.'

Pat Ryan stiffened. 'Into town, you say, how long are they gone?'

'They were late enough going, I am afraid, so they should be having tea in O'Briens about now. Tea and cakes, my Missis has a sweet tooth, you know.'

'Lord above man why did you let them go today? Didn't you know about the siege?'

'What are you saying man? What siege?'

'The bridge is going up this very hour. The Freestaters are on Mount Misery and the Republicans are raising the bridge against them.'

Ernest dropped the cleaver from his hand and began fumbling with his apron.

'What can I do man, what can I do? You know these people Mr Ryan. You can speak to them. Tell them to let my Missis and the child come across.'

Pat Ryan drew a deep breath and seemed to withdraw into himself. 'What are you saying man? How would I know them or have any influence with them?'

Ernest paused and looked up slowly. 'Mr Ryan I am not stupid. I notice things. I can't help it. Now you must help me or my Missis and child could be killed.'

Pat Ryan dropped his pretence and told him to get the pony and trap yoked up at once. Together they worked and as they turned to trot out of the courtyard Ernst called out 'What about the pig?'

Pat stooped and hoisted the pig into the trap.

'Never mind the bloody pig. He is a Republican, like myself. Move it man, move it.'

Sion Row was crowded as they turned off the Rockshire Road, heading for the bridge. People shouted at them to turn back, that there was shooting at the bridge. Ernest was like a man possessed; he urged the pony forward against the running crowd. Pat stood up in the trap trying vainly to see if he could spot any sign of the woman and child.

'I can't see anyone in this crowd. What was she wearing man?' he shouted at Ernest.

'A hat man, she was wearing a blue hat, with a peacock's feather in it.'

They were round the bend now, above the bridge, and could hear and see the fleeing people and Pat called out to a woman as they passed. He asked if she had seen Mrs Evans and the boy, but she answered no and that she hoped they were safe on the other side.

When they could go no further Pat urged Ernest to pull into the side and let the pony stand. They would try and get to his little boat, which he always left near the bridge. Without thinking he grabbed the pig and took him with him. They managed to get to the boat before the shooting started up again.

With the pig squealing, in the bottom of the boat, the two men began to row across under cover of the bridge. Ernest, with the heat of battle on him, began to sing 'Men of Harlech', and in spite of himself. Pat Ryan smiled. Pigwig grunted.

It was Davy who saw them first and shouted at Ma that someone was coming over in a little boat, and maybe they would take them across. Ma insisted on waiting on the edge of the quay just below the bridge. Then she heard the Welsh voice raised in battle hymn and she shouted. 'Ernest, Ernest, we are here, over here. Thank God you have come, you dear, dear man.'

The sergeant shouted at her to get down or she would be killed and she ducked down onto the slip, drawing Davy with her. The Sergeant ordered his men to hold their fire and then Davy cried out, 'Ma, Ma they have Pigwig with them. It's Pat Ryan and Pigwig.'

'Well, bless my soul,' said the sergeant 'It is Pat Ryan, and the pig still lives. Hold your fire men.'

There was a little bit of scraping against the stonework, muttered curses, followed by a desperate clinging on and shuffling before they got the woman and boy into the boat.

The boat rocked savagely when Mrs Evans tried to embrace her husband, and they all shouted at her to be still and not have them over. Davy took the pig in his arms and Pat Ryan called out to the sergeant to give them covering fire as they crossed back. Da said that he would have a ham for every man if they kept them from getting shot as they rowed back. Oh, he was in fine form, now that he had his Missis and boy with him again.

'Come on men', shouted the sergeant, 'give them covering fire'. Then, in spite of the danger, a great cheer went up when the sergeant called out 'Evans for meat and Dev for the Republic.'

They were almost across safely when a shot rang out, from the rocky outcrop above the river. The boy and pig screamed in unison. Blood spurted. Ma cried out 'Oh Davy, Davy, have they killed you?' And she tried to get to him, rocking the boat badly.

'Son, son, where are you shot?' cried Ernest.

'The bastards, to shoot a child!' said Pat Ryan, shocked to the core.

Then there was a little moan and a gasp and Davy spoke. 'Da, Da, you can give them the ham now. Poor Pigwig is dead.' And he burst into tears as the blood drained away, in the bottom of the boat, from the Republican Pig.

It was the size of Pigwig, him being a White York, that had saved Davy, Da said. Davy no longer cared, nor did he want to be a butcher anymore. He fancied himself now avenging the death of Pigwig and planned to be a soldier with the biggest gun ever.

The siege of Waterford in July 1922 changed the world of many and to this very day people recall, with bitterness, how family members were split and never again regained that camaraderie they knew before.

# 30

# THE TUNNEL BENEATH THE RIVER SUIR

We were often told that long ago, in troubled times, and there were many such times in Waterford's history, the merchants and clergy got together and decided it would be a great idea to dig out a tunnel under the River Suir. The idea was that if those in the city needed to get away from a besieging enemy they could cross over through the tunnel and come out in the grounds or indeed inside in the abbey on the Ferrybank side and vice versa.

The location of the tunnel entrance in the city was never specified except that some believed it came up near Reginald's Tower and some that it came up near Christ Church Cathedral.

Whether they had the technology to do such a thing or not is debatable but it was widely believed that it was not only possible but was done.

The further addition to this story was that, during the 'Troubles', someone discovered the entrance to the tunnel and started into the depths with some companions. They had little light and were scared witless in case the River Suir would come down on top of them and there were spiders and cobwebs the like of which they had never seen before. Also there were scurryings and half-seen movements all around them and the air was musty and damp.

They decided to turn back, all except one, who, despite warnings from his companions, chose to carry on investigating. Well, need I tell you, the story goes, that he was never seen again and no one dared to investigate any deeper into the tunnel. But a dog did once run down it and came back with a human bone. So they say. No name was ever even suggested to go along with this mysterious disappearance nor did any of us ask, for fear it might be someone we knew.

We were always told that there were rats down there as big as dogs and they would surely eat a man let alone a youngster.

The following account of the same tale was told by an old man who seemed to know more than he should but when we questioned him he tapped the side of his nose and said 'I'm saying nothing'. But this is what he told us.

There was a young man once and his name was Murphy. He came from the right side of the bridge, as they say, meaning Ferrybank. There was another name for Ferrybank once; it was called The Slip because of all the shipbuilding that went on there. Young Murphy was interested in all things mysterious and spent a lot of time with his head in books.

It was no wonder then that he stumbled upon a tale which was to stir him up to take action eventually. This was no foreign or fanciful tale, as far as he could tell, and it was entirely possible. Waterford had been invaded and besieged many times so the secreting away of valuable items of Church and State was common practice and he was sure that not all of it had been recovered yet. Sure didn't people who hid things often get killed, and he was right in that.

He spent some more time trying to get a look at old maps and records held by Waterford Corporation, on the pretence of writing about history, so no one paid much mind to Murphy and his comings and goings. If they did notice him the called him The Professor and smiled.

Three weeks into his research he withdrew from the public eye and appeared content to live his life with his head in a book.

But Murphy's heart was all of a flutter. He had found a mystery on his own doorstep and only he could put the pieces together. He lived alone since both his parents were lost to TB, which was rife at the time. In the quiet of his own kitchen, as the sunset, he lit the oil lamp and brought it to the table. His next step was to remove a very old piece of vellum from between the pages of his book. This he had appropriated during his perusal of the old maps in the Corporation's oldest files. He fully intended to give it back, when he was finished with it. He would slip it back into the old leather pouch, covered in dust and cobwebs, down at the side of the press, and no one would ever know it had been out of the room.

Now all he had to do was make it correspond to the Waterford he knew in his time. The river still flowed in the same manner so it shouldn't be hard, but which building was which now was another problem.

There was no bridge marked on the map but Reginald's Tower was clearly indicated. So was Kilculliheen Abbey on the other side of the river and another place, further back. The church, marked with a cross had to be Christ Church, or maybe the Friary. There were one or two other squiggles which were smudged and could not be made out at all.

He spent a long time studying the old map and trying to interpret the directions written in faded ink at the side. He was sure the map lead to buried treasure. He was positive it led to hidden artefacts, maybe golden chalices or other items of immense value. Why else would there be a big X marking different places. Everyone knows that X marks the spot. He decided that he needed someone to confide in. It was too big a responsibility for him to take on alone and if any digging or heavy lifting needed to be done he was not suited to that kind of labour.

Now you and I know the way of secrets. If more than one person knows you might as well take out a full page add in the *Munster Express* or the *News & Star*. Word got around quite quickly that Murphy had found a treasure map and he might need a little bit of help. This was a cause for jeering, for no one thought very highly of 'Murphy the Book'. Only Flynner, who was always on the outside of things looking in, much the same as Murphy himself, agreed to meet with him and take a chance it might be genuine. The others waited and watched.

There was no electric light then so Murphy gathered his candles and matches and even got a little Tilly Lamp for an emergency. It was early in the evening when he started out on his adventures. He was to meet Flynner down by the Boat Club and they would bide their time and slip over the Abbey wall into the graveyard, when no one was looking, and following the directions on the map they would unearth the buried treasure.

The plan seemed sound but the first thing Murphy noticed was that there seemed to be an awful lot of lads hanging around the Boat Club. Eventually he got fed up waiting – the map was burning a hole in his pocket – so he gave Flynner the beck and the two of them walked back up the lane, as though they were going home, and they slipped in the gate of the Abbey instead.

Murphy thought his heart would leap out of his chest, so excited did he feel. Flynner kept looking around and was very jumpy, starting at every sound. He had never been in a Protestant graveyard before, sure anything could happen. They got to the shelter of the abbey wall and checked the map again. They stepped out the paces as best they could from the riverside of the graveyard. It was getting darker by the minute and the overhanging trees didn't help with all their rustling and shadow casting.

They were intent now on their adventure and were more than a little disappointed when they came to a flat table-like gravestone each time they counted. They sat on it and wondered where they went wrong and decided to count again. The sounds in the graveyard were increasing and there was a rustling and movement all around them.

The Tilly Lamp had to be lit this time so they wouldn't fall over anything as they paced and counted. As the wick took light, both of them nearly jumped out of their skins. A loud scraping sound echoed around the graveyard and birds fluttered, away out of the trees above them. Flynner gave a little croak and his hand gripped Murphy's arm.

'Did you hear that?' he gulped.

'Probably a slate coming off the roof with the birds', whispered Murphy.

'Yea, yea, that's what it was.' Flynner let go his arm and they began to walk forward, counting softly. Two seconds later Murphy let out a yell as he back pedalled into Flynner. The Slab had been lifted and now sat askew across the grave. 'Oh heart of God we're finished altogether', gasped Flynner. Sounds of movement came from all around them. Soft rustling like feet walking, whispers, and something that sounded halfway between a giggle and a scream.

Murphy, thinking on his feet, grabbed Flynner and the two of them went headlong into the uncovered grave. If whoever owned this grave was out and about then the safest place to hide was inside. They could hide in it until the daylight came, he reasoned. But he was not going to meet any ghosts walking around that night. All went quiet and by the light of the little Tilly Lamp they saw that they were not in a grave at all but the start of a tunnel of some sorts. Just as they made this discovery they heard the stone slab being shoved back in place above them.

Terror gripped them and they shouted and screamed and hammered but all they heard was laughter echoing back at them.

When the first wave of terror passed they decided that they might as well see where the tunnel would lead to; maybe they could escape at the other end.

It was dank and musty and seemed to lead them down and down. Here and there water dripped and pooled. The little lamp began to flicker and its light dwindled slowly. Clutching each other, all thoughts of the treasure gone, they began to move, step by careful step, stumbling and weeping with fright as strange gurgling noises seemed to come from all around them.

Something brushed against Murphy's leg and he screamed. He thought he heard another scream echo way back behind him. They dared not stop. Flynner took the lead now and they lighted one of the little candles from his pocket. It flickered alarmingly and the air was thick around them. Prayers began to come involuntarily to their lips.

The prayers were interspersed with curses for their own stupidity. Fear of death dogged every step. The water seemed to be getting deeper now and was up almost to their knees. Flynner dropped the candle as something fluttered past his head. With chattering teeth and shaking hands they somehow managed to light another stub of candle.

'It has to come out somewhere', said Murphy. 'It just has to.' Ten more steps and the water seemed to get less again and they were climbing up, and up a gradual rise. If anything the air was worse here and the skittering and movement seemed increased.

Thinking that they might never see God's good light again they struggled wearily on. Sometimes they had to climb over old timbers and mounds of earth to get past. When Flynner banged his head on the roof of the tunnel they stopped. They listened. Faint noises came to them.

'Footsteps, and voices, can you hear them?' Murphy cried out in relief.

It took them another fifteen desperate minutes to find a way out. They came out in a church crypt but they could see a crack of light up the steps and they ran, stumbling, towards it. When they burst forth from the crypt there were screams and shouts of alarm from the group gathered there.

They didn't care. They were safe. The guns on the table didn't scare them. Nothing would ever scare them again.

The cold feel of the revolver pressed to his cheek somehow steadied him. He smiled and smiled. Flynner giggled like a child and hugged the man with the gun.

It took them a long while to make sense to the people around them. Murphy handed them his map with the X marks the spot on it and another candle was lit so everyone could see it clearly.

Some men took candles and guns and went back down through the crypt. Nothing anyone could say or do would persuade either Murphy or Flynner to go with them. Someone gave the two lads a swig of whiskey. Never having had it before it went straight to their heads and both slumped quietly down against the wall.

It was a long time later when someone knocked twice on the room door. The party who had gone down the tunnel were back. They were grim-faced and dirty. They had found their way through they said, across under the river and scared a group of young men and women half to death.

The jokers had slid the slab off the grave and never checked inside it in the dark so when Murphy and Flynner disappeared into it they slid the stone over as a joke intending to move it in a few minutes but when they did move it the two lads had vanished. Then before they could decide who to call, up came a group of armed men from the same grave. Terror was the name of the game.

In the days that followed they were sworn to secrecy and now lived in darker world than they had known before. They never spoke about what happened that night and no one else did either. The fact that their hair had turned grey over night was noted but not commented on. Speculation about a tunnel was forgotten and those who knew left it so.

# 31

# HANS
# MUFF

Glass-blowing businesses had existed in Waterford since 1783 when it was started up by two brothers, George and William Penrose. That first glass company fell on hard times and closed in 1851.

In 1947 a Czech immigrant by the name of Charles Bacik established a glass works in Johnstown, Waterford. He was joined by a fellow countryman Miroslav Havel, who was a glass designer. Times were difficult as the Second World War had just ended and Ireland was struggling, like the rest of Europe, to get back to some sort of normality. The little Waterford Glass company was taken over first by Irish Glass Bottle Co.

One of the new owners, Joseph McGrath, became a much-loved figure to the workforce and under his stewardship the factory thrived and was a good place to work. However, the time came when, the now firmly established on world markets Waterford Glass, changed hands again. For many of the older workers this was the beginning of the end. The new regime was all about profit and workers were asked to adapt to new rules and regulations, made by people who had never worked glass.

Every craft has its own traditions and folklore. The glass makers who came from Europe to Waterford, in the early days, brought with them their ancient traditions and tales and this particular piece of folklore in the glass-making world was kept to themselves. Only a glass blower would know about Hans Muff.

This story is about the time when it became evident that things were going from bad to worse for the workers. The men who knew molten glass in all its moods were gone. The men who had brought old traditions like the making of spaghetti bolognaise in cans resting up on the hot surface of the furnace and cooking fresh-caught fish wrapped in tinfoil in the same manner, were no longer struggling to learn English beside the locals in the blowing rooms. The old storytellers of the craft no longer spoke softly about the dreaded Hans Muff.

The squad car slowed as it passed him the second time around. The driver looked towards his partner and frowned. 'What do you think Ned? Is he or isn't he?'

Ned turned himself around, looking back over the seats at the silent, immobile figure, shrugged and turned forward again. 'It's hard to tell. He doesn't look drunk to me. Maybe he's just pissin'.'

The driver grinned, 'Let's hope so. You heard what the Sergeant said "If they're standing still looking into the river they're either pissin' or thinking of jumping" and he's never wrong. Look, we'll give another turn up through the town and then if he's still here when we come back we'll have a word.' The car indicator winked orange and they turned away from the quayside into the evening traffic.

Pat didn't notice them. He didn't even notice the water which surged, brown and restless past his feet. He was thirty-two years away, in a manner of speaking.

It was his first job, his first day at work, his first step into a man's world and God, was he scared. Only out of short pants a wet day and here he was, a day off sixteen. John Kennedy had waited out-side the factory gate for him and walked with him across the yard. 'Pat', said he, 'never mind what they shout at you or call you, just get on with the work as best you can and before you know it you'll be doing it with your eyes closed.'

Well he got used to it, eventually, but he never in all his years managed to do it with his eyes closed, neither did anyone else that he knew of. It was much too dangerous.

He smelled the heat before he felt it. It surged out at them in waves as they went into the blowing room. Noise rushed hotly behind the heat. Men shouted and sweat dripped and by God, he nearly ran then. He was scared witless but if he let it get a hold on him he would never face anyone again. Everyone here knew everyone else, probably knew him too but he couldn't tell. He found it hard to focus on the faces which he knew were all turned towards him from the various levels on the work floor. He had to stand his ground. Then the supervisor came busily towards him and there was no turning back.

Put to carry the red hot, new-blown glass to the lehr so it would cool slowly, he was frightened. Not the same kind of fear which had gripped him as he came in but a new gut-gnawing fear that he would either hold it too tightly between the callipers and distort the blown shape before he reached the lehr or worst of all drop it through holding it too lightly and God knows the weight of some of the bloody things was awful on his skinny boy's arms.

The distance from the furnace to the lehr at the other end of the floor seemed miles and this he traversed over and over again carrying carefully, scurrying back, dodging the clip on the ear from the men who thought he was not moving fast enough or carefully enough, running, sweating until the ire on the insides of his thighs made it a living hell.

Then the hooter blew. Never, never again he thought, but once outside the gates with the fresh breeze from the river blowing up between the rows of houses it didn't seem so bad. He had got through his first day. Learned the names of the tools of the trade, the irons, the moulds, sat with the men over mugs of tea and unbelievably, heard some of them sing as they worked in that stifling heat. They were happy in that place.

That night he soaped the ire on his thighs and dabbed metholated spirits on it. His father had read in some First Aid book that this was the thing to do. He lay in the dark, on top of his bed, with his legs apart to get comfortable but when he heard his brother Jim come in later on he scrambled for his pyjama bottom and got under the bedclothes.

After that it was work every day and he learned by trial and error. Some of the Master Craftsmen were only too willing to teach him how they worked the molten glass while others neither had the inclination nor the talent to teach anyone. But he soon sorted out whom he could ask questions and who to avoid. He graduated from being 'knocker off', which was what he was called in the beginning, to being a 'bit gatherer' and he proudly bore the scorch marks along his forearm which now proclaimed him as a glass worker. It was about this time when he first heard of the elusive Hans Muff.

Sitting hunched over the mugs of steaming tea at the lunch break he heard them talk about Ger. Ger was the man whose place he had taken as a bit gatherer. 'Oh he's bad all right', remarked one. The others nodded. 'Once I heard him say he'd seen Hans Muff I knew he was finished. You can't work the glass once you start seeing him.'

He remembered looking carefully from one to the other of the men but he kept his mouth shut. He had learned by then that they often 'set up' the younger lads so they would ask something stupid and by God there was no way he was going to give them a laugh at his expense. However, he couldn't help wondering and sometimes when he was on edge about something else altogether, this thought would rise at the back of his mind that this was the day he might see the dreaded Hans Muff.

Down through the years, by careful listening he learned that this was what some of the men who were hard on the drink or suffering with the nerves came to imagine they saw at the back of the furnace dancing on the molten glass – a little man, some said he was green, others red or blue but it always had the same result: they finished up the job.

He never saw Hans Muff but there were worse things to be met on the work floor in those days. Some of the supervisors would grind you into the dirt if you let them. Bastards! And they not knowing the first thing about molten glass. Not like the old days when everyone could turn their hand to the work and if they saw you do something wrong, they could show you how to do it right. Today they were smart college boys who only knew how to cut to

the quick with a smart comment and never boasted a blister the size of a half crown on their hands. By God they couldn't. They didn't know which end of the iron should be caught.

The squad car came slowly around again and pulled up beside the paper shop across the quay. They looked at him. He hadn't moved. 'What do you think? Is it make your mind up time or not?'

The driver shrugged, 'Well he sure can't be pissin' all that time.'

Ned grinned. 'Too right. I'll ramble over so. Keep an eye let you.'

Pat felt the familiar churning in his gut. He shouldn't let them do that to him. The ulcer would only act up again. Better put the supervisors out of his mind or he'd end up bleeding inside. Mary would have a fit if that happened again. God help her, she was great for managing. Sometimes she got tired of people, even her own, blast them, telling her how well off she was and they not knowing how little he was bringing in.

Just because he was in the glass they assumed that the wages were good. Well they weren't. Not for the blowers, ever. They had always been treated as second class to the cutters even though they were the ones making the glass but no one outside ever knew that. The blowers had some pride. Well it was decision time now and that was all about it. There was no way he could meet the mortgage repayments and the other commitments.

Ned cleared his throat and leaned companionable against the railing. Pat, startled out of his deep thoughts, twitched nervously, his hand going to his stomach which twitched correspondingly. He winced and stared at the Garda.

'What! Sorry, did you say something?'

Ned shook his head slowly, his eyes followed the movement of the hand, 'Ulcers', he thought. He noted the streaked burn marks on the forearm and knew he had a glass worker.

'Just stopping off for a quick drag, want one?' He proffered the cigarette packet. He saw the hand begin to reach then Pat withdrew it sharply.

'No, no I'd better not. It might only start me off again.' He sighed and turned back to meditating the river. 'They're the devil to give up you know.'

Ned nodded his agreement and drew heavily on the cigarette, feeling at a loss. He knew the position in the glass. Knew the state some of the poor devils were in trying to make ends meet. You'd rarely meet a glass worker up in the barracks these days. Oh before you'd meet them all right, mostly when they wanted a passport fixed up for the holidays or such like, but not many were going on holidays now.

'Oh hard times'.

They both started as he said the words out loud, not meaning to.

Pat turned a curious glance in his direction.

'Christ! I've gone and done it now', thought Ned. 'I'll drive the poor oul sod over the edge if he's not there already, me and me mouth.'

Then Pat began to chuckle softly beside him. The chuckle grew to a great big bubble of a laugh which was so infectious that Ned found himself responding to the merriment and they doubled over laughing as they stood on the brim of the river.

Pat, wiped his eyes and grinned at him. 'You know when you said that, about the "hard times" you gave me an awful start. Me poor Father used to say that all the time, God be good to him, and you even sounded like him.'

Ned blew out a long stream of smoke. Relief flowing through him. 'I'm glad of that then. You know there's nothing like a good laugh to make you feel better.'

Pat turned and smiled warmly, really looking at him for the first time. He saw the long lean jaw of the man beside him and the compassionate look in his eye and for some reason he no longer felt desperate.

'I've been standing here this past hour or more you know, trying to decide ...'

He paused and Ned drew hard on the fag. 'This is it', he thought. He said nothing and the glassman didn't seem to want him to either, he just stared unseeingly out over the water. There was no tension about him, Ned noticed and relaxed again until he remembered the Sergeant telling them how potential suicides usually became very calm once they decided to go. Ned shifted position so he would be ready to act. He threw the stub of the cigarette into the water.

Pat watched the arc of it as it flared and flew then bobbed away on the tide. A tiny Hans Muff, he thought, as it passed him by, an omen maybe, then he shook his head.

'You should give them up', he said quietly.

'I know, I know', Ned replied quickly, wondering at the back of his mind if these were the last words. People always seemed to ask 'Did he say anything before he went?' Ned smiled to himself as he wondered what they'd make of this.

'It's a fierce dirty river', he said.

Pat seemed to focus on the water for the first time and once again Ned regretted his words.

'There's been a lot of "jumpers" lately I hear.'

Tension tightened Ned's throat. 'Aye', he said, then, cautiously 'but none of them glass workers mind you.'

Pat's eyes came round to meet his again, a smile hovering behind them. 'I suppose you know the reason for that?' Ned drew a breath slowly and thought about it, yes, the answer was safe enough if anything it would help.

'Sure the poor devils can't even do that. They'd be no insurance for the wives if they did.'

Pat nodded, 'Now you have it. You know I was just thinking before you came along that in a matter of two years they managed to destroy what it took me thirty two hard years to learn. The expertise, the craft, the pride, the loyalty ...' He stopped. Choked up on the words and turned his face to the river.

Ned fumbled with the cigarettes and lit up. Then Pat began to speak again. 'You know there was a time when we used to sing as we worked. It was funny really, all the lads stripped to waist, sweat drippin' down off them, heat blasting out at them, blowing, shaping, making and they singing like the bloody Vienna Boys Choir. There was one time, oh a long, long time ago when I remember we even had a Sing Out. Two of the lads trying to better one another singing and we all stopped work to hear them.' He sighed sadly.

Ned didn't move. He watched the flutter of the short sleeves on Pat's shirt in the light summer breeze and waited.

'Blowers die fairly young you know', Pat stated matter-of-factly. 'It's the lead, the constant blowing, hot air into the lungs or something like that.' He did not mention Hans Muff, that was glass lore.

He turned and looked at Ned. 'You know, I don't know one single Blower who lived to be old. Can you imagine that?'

Ned shook his head. 'Old Gardaí never die', he said slowly and smiled.

Pat looked at him, 'God help them so', he said but he understood exactly what Ned meant. 'It should be like that for us as well. The glass gets into the blood. The mouldin' and the shapin' the pure joy of seeing a piece come out right, not too thick or too thin. Ah you'd want to work the molten glass and it honey red to know what I mean ...' His voice tailed away and the two men sighed, one for the knowing and the other at the lack of it.

Ned looked again at the man beside him and decided to take a chance. 'You're not thinking of going in I hope?' he said half joking, half in earnest. Pat shook his head but he didn't laugh. 'That would be the easy way, wouldn't it? Leave the troubles to someone else. Naw, I'll have a talk with herself and we'll manage somehow in spite of them and their multinationals.' There was a deep sadness behind the words rather than the bitterness Ned expected.

He shook his head slowly, 'I wish I could help, tell you it will be all right or something like that'. He paused and his eyes met Pat's. 'Listen, if you ever need to have a chat give me a shout. Just ring the station and ask for Ned. I'm the only "Ned" up there and sure if nothing else we can talk about hard times.' The two men grinned in companionship at one another.

'Maybe I will', said Pat and he straightened his shoulders. 'Maybe I will.'

The handset crackled and they heard the station calling for someone to go to an accident scene. Ned took a last quick drag on the cigarette and flicked it into the water. 'I'd better be off. It sounds bad.'

Pat nodded. 'I'll be off in a minute myself I just want to have a quick piss.' He wondered why Ned laughed all the way back to the car.

There are many stories told about glass workers and in Waterford and the surrounding areas. You would always know a glass worker by his sense of humour. It was a humour all of its own.

One story goes about the wife of a certain worker who seeing the TV detector van in the street told the man in the van that if he called to her house, giving the number, that he should tell her husband that the TV licence was behind the clock on the mantelpiece. The TV man eventually knocked on the door of the house and the husband answered it. 'God boy, sure I don't know where the licence is at all' says he. 'No worries at all says the TV man, it's behind the clock on the mantelpiece'.

'Go on,' says the glass man, 'I didn't know you could see into the houses with that thing on the van.'

Another worker, whose wife, after many long years, gave birth to a son, proudly showed off his heir only to be told 'Sure he can't be yours at all.' Thunderstruck, the proud father asked, 'How do you make that out.' The answer was simple 'Sure, your hair is as grey as a badger and that child, has lovely black hair.'

# 32

# ST CUAN'S WELL AND
# THE SACRED TROUT

*There are stories all around the world and in different cultures which
have the same kind of theme. This story, which was given to me by
a lady from Mothel, Breda Mears, is very similar to the Rian Bó
Phadraig story. In fact both the stories have the rascal coming across
the mountains to do the dastardly deed. In Rian Bó Phadraig the thief
comes over the Knockmealdown Mountains and the thief in Mothel
comes either over the Comeraghs or the Monavullagh Mountains.*

Mothel, in Co. Waterford, is a name which echoes down through the
centuries as a place of great holiness and people have journeyed there
for help and healing since St Brogan first set foot on the grassy slopes. It
is a high place with beautiful scenery. St Brogan's first attempt at setting
up home there was, as it was the custom then, a modest monk's cell.

There was life in Mothel long before St Brogan, St Cuan or
even St Patrick himself were heard of. There is a Dolmen in the
field below that of the holy well which bears testament to this.
Our ancient ancestors seemed to have a love of high and beautiful
places. There is little trace left now of their passing.

However, St Brogan was the 'whole man' in the early days of
Mothel, and is credited with bringing Christianity to the tribes of
the surrounding area. He lived, by all accounts, in and around the

same time as St Patrick and some people even go as far as to say that the good man was a nephew of St Patrick, but sure who knows now. It is enough for us to know that he was a great man and did God's work in this lovely, ancient place.

He had a fellow saint who joined him in his endeavours, in Mothel, and he was named St Cuan. They met each other, we are told, in Co. Wexford and he too came to Mothel, inspired by the same desire to spread Christianity to the local tribes. They set up near the Holy Well but they were soon joined by others, of like mind, and so it expanded into a little monastery.

It must have been very successful for it is mentioned in many old records and eventually, hundreds of years later, a new monastery was built higher up, away from the Holy Well. This was a thriving Augustinian Monastery known as Mothel Abbey.

Well, St Brogan and St Cuan were famous for different things. St Cuan was connected more to the Holy Well, it seems, and St Brogan, who was described as a 'scribe', was probably better suited to running their little monastery. Whatever their talents, the two saints agreed to dedicate the holy well to the Holy Mother, the Blessed Virgin Mary. Lord only knows to whom it was dedicated before their coming. The belief in its healing power must have always been there, for people were closer to the workings of nature and the sacredness of water in those times.

The story I want to tell you was, I am told, handed down by oral tradition, so it has come many hundreds of years, through many voices, to reach us.

The holy well is in the townland of Ballynevin and is a basin of crystal water, about 8 feet in diameter and approximately 8 feet deep. Today, it still bubbles up the pure healing water which flows out at the lower side and a little stream trickles down the green hillside to run along by a wall where you will find two little pillars of stone standing upright and slab steps leading down to the flowing water. A little further on it joins with a bigger stream which flows strongly away.

Overhanging the well there is an ancient Ash tree which is ridged and runneled along its silver grey bark. Both the tree and the well seem joined in their sacredness, or maybe that is just imagination.

The tree and the well are cared for and large branches have been taken from the ancient Ash at some time. It is possible that these branches would have tipped the tree into the well, had this not been done, for the great trunk of the ash slants in over the water.

There was a time when this holy well was inhabited by a 'sacred trout' which was highly regarded and in some cases even venerated by the locals. They would never dream of harming or even touching a scale of the 'sacred trout', so you can imagine their horror and dismay when a smart young man took it into his head to appropriate the creature from the holy well.

God alone knows what can have been in his mind. Maybe he wanted it to cure someone or maybe he did not want it for any reason other than to torment the locals. Whatever his reason, he took off with the captured 'sacred trout', with his feet hitting the ground in spots, and the whole neighbourhood giving chase.

It is said that he came 'from beyond the mountain' and it was in that direction he headed with his stolen trophy. He ran without stopping for the pass of Bealavallaig until, on the point of being caught, and for fear of his life, he dropped the precious fish.

Whether the *cratur* survived this ordeal, or not, there is no record, just a lengthy pause in the telling.

The cures attributed to this healing well are not set down or recorded although the healing of ailments of the eyes has been mentioned. Some say that the healing of the heart, either physical or emotional, was possible also. If people found peace there, in that serene high place, then that indeed was a cure also.

There is a Pattern Day held in Mothel every year on the Sunday nearest to 8 July to commemorate St Brogan and St Cuan and in honour of the Blessed Virgin.

There is a little booklet, *The Story of Mothel* written by Very Revd P. Canon Power, D.Litt, still doing the rounds in Clonea Parish. This booklet gives a more precise and detailed historical background, for those interested in historical fact.

## The Ash Tree

The tradition of the holy trees is as old as that of the holy wells. There is an ancient and separate folklore attached to trees.

In some counties people still carry on old traditions of placing offerings or pieces of coloured cloths or ribbons on the branches of these trees. Some people hang Rosary beads and medals. They place them there in the hope of healing or in thanksgiving for favours received. This is still carried on, in some areas of Co. Waterford but not at the site in Mothel.

The Ash is one of the 'noble trees' and is used in the first Irish alphabet – Ogam or Ogham. The Ash represents the land goddess, fertility and healing. Three of the Five Great Trees of Ireland were ash trees. They were located around the centre of Ireland in the long ago time, acting as guardians and protectors of the whole land. The Ash also stands for renewal as it quickly sends out new growth when cut down. Because of this capability it is known as a Tree of Life.

Ash trees were used in weather forecasting. If the Oak leafed first dry weather would follow; if the Ash leafed first wet weather was forecast.

In ancient times the young fresh leaves of the Ash were used as a type of tea for treatment of gout, jaundice and rheumatism.

All right, I will mention it so – the Ash is what the hurleys used by the men of the Deise, are made from.

## HOLY TREES IN CO. WATERFORD

Holy trees were believed to be due to a miracle of the local saint. An example of this is St Colman's sacred tree in 'the old parish' three miles north of Ardmore, Co. Waterford. The story is that as St Colman was walking near his old church, he stuck a little dry stick in the ground. The stick took root and grew into a tree which never can be destroyed. This type of story is told about many sacred trees around Ireland and in Europe.

## ST DECLAN'S WELL AT TOOR, AGLISH, CO. WATERFORD

Local tradition has it that St Declan stopped at this holy well to quench his thirst and, by so doing, his blessing was given to the water therein. In the long ago time this area was densely forested, so at that time the holy well would have been surrounded by trees, but they are long gone now and instead of a holy tree with its usual attachments you will find a small bush which is adorned with ribbons, pieces of cloth, rosary beads and other items which people have left by way of prayer or thanksgiving.

## AT ST DECLAN'S WELL IN ARDMORE THERE IS NO SACRED TREE.

Sometimes, trees, in particular, Hawthorn trees, are classed as holy or sacred, not because a saint has touched them but because of the ancient belief in nature and Fairy Folk. There are many places in Co. Waterford where farmers will not disturb a particular Hawthorn Tree or a group of Hawthorn or Oak trees. This is from an ancient and primal knowing that to do so would be harmful, one way or another.

It is considered very unlucky to bring the Hawthorn blossoms inside the house. On the other hand, its leaves and fruit (Melahave) are edible and are used as an all-purpose cardiac tonic and some say it is great for varicose veins.

On the road going up to the Comeragh Mountains there was a Hawthorn tree (the Fairy Tree), which was bedecked with all sorts of items and was believed to bring good health or fortune to those who stopped there to pray or wish.

Unfortunately, in recent times some dark soul took it upon themselves to cut down this tree, which harmed none, but gave hope to many. I understand that some locals have got together to plant a replacement tree on the site.

At around the same place as the Fairy Tree, on the road to Mahon Falls, there is a section of the road which is known as the Magic Road.

After you cross the first cattle-grid on this journey you come to a downhill grade. At the bottom of this hill stop your car and you will be astounded to find that your car begins to move back up the hill without any help from you. The experts say that this is caused by some electro-magnetic energy in the earth at this point but for myself, I like to believe in magic.


## Oak Groves

You will see many Oak groves around Co. Waterford, and in the woodlands there are still certain areas where you will find old Oak trees grouped together, in circular formation. There is a tradition that if you carry an acorn on your person or keep one in your home that it will bring good luck.

The Druids held their meetings and ceremonies in the ancient Oak groves because of the power and protection the Oak provided. Oak is used in the building of churches also.

# 33

# THE
# GLAS GAIBHNEACH

*Uair amháin, fadó fadó,* many centuries before the invention of milking machines and quotas, there roamed through the lush pastures of Munster a cow. Her name was neither Daisy nor Bluebell, she was called the *Glas Gaibhneach* – and she was no ordinary cow. So capacious was her udder that it was said that any vessel she was milked into would be filled to the brim before it ran dry. Fortunately, neither supertankers nor cold storage were known in those days, or who knows to what indignities this generous animal might have been subjected. Certainly she had no difficulty with the ordinary bucket, pail, kieve or cask.

The *Glas Gaibhneach* paid many visits to the Déise. There are traditions of her presence at Ballycommera in the parish of Grange, whence she wandered to Ardmore and thence to Ferry Point. At Seafield near Bunmahon is Gleann an Earbaill – the glen of the tail – a stream channel that was scooped out by her long trailing tail as she munched her way towards Carrigcastle. Another time she spent a night in the little parish of Lickoran, a second night at Newcastle, and a third at Glenanore, departing thence via the Gap to Rathgormack. Sheegouna in the parish of Garrangibbon is named after her. And so fertile did she find Páirc an Iarla in the townland of Killune near Tramore that she patronised it for several nights.

Indeed, this generous beast might still be with us today had it not been for the ungrateful cynicism of a farmer's wife in Ballylaneen, who devised an ingenious method of testing the tradition that the *Glas Gaibhneach*'s udder would never run dry. So long did the milking take that, having submitted patiently for several hours, the *Glas Gaibhneach* looked round to see what was happening, only to find that she was being milked into a sieve! Is there no end to the curiosity of a woman?

Now, if there is one thing a lady can't stand, it's the feeling that another lady is taking the mickey out of her. With one belt of her hind legs the *Glas Gaibhneach* sent the sieve and its owner flying into the nearest slurry pit. She then stalked out of the milking parlour with her eyes blazing and her voice rising from her usual gentle lowing to an ominous bellow. As a sign of further displeasure she stuck her horns in the ground and left a trench behind her that bore an uncanny resemblance to the R677 (though with fewer potholes). The grinding of her teeth left a trail of loose chippings. Nor did she stop till she reached Bunmahon, where she plunged into the sea, leaving a wake after her that swamped a thousand holiday caravans.

And from that day to this there has been no sign of the *Glas Gaibhneach. Nach mór an trua é.'*

*Main source: P. Canon Power,* Place Names of Decies *(1952 edition), pp. 92, 119, 160, 259, 351, 368. This story was passed on to me from Julian Walton, folklorist, Waterford.*